A Wind on the Heath

James Pattinson

Chapter
Chapter
Chapter
Chapter
Chapter
Chapter
Chapter
Chapter
Chapter
Chapter
Chapter
Chapter
Chapter
Chapter
Chapter
Chapter
Chapter
Chapter
Chapter
Chapter
Chapter
Chapter
Chapter
Chapter

Chapter Twenty-Six – CELEBRATION	141
Chapter Twenty-Seven – SPLIT	147
Chapter Twenty-Eight – TRYST	151
Chapter Twenty-Nine – MURDER	156

Chapter One – MEDITATION

When Sterne glanced out of the window he could see Peter and Petra meditating in the garden. He was looking down on them from a higher level, since his flat was on the first floor; and in fact he rented it from the couple below, who owned the house and occupied the ground floor themselves.

The garden was at the rear of the house, and it was little more than a patch of weedy grass which was only occasionally trimmed with a racketing hand-propelled mower. Overgrown privet hedges on three sides afforded a certain degree of privacy; and this was just as well, seeing that Peter and Petra liked to do their meditation in the nude whenever the weather allowed them to do so without too much discomfort from the chill. As it did now in these dying days of summer.

Despite the screen of privet, they were of course visible from the upper windows of other houses in the terrace, but this appeared not to bother them. They were remarkably unself-conscious regarding their naked bodies, which were not in any case of a kind to attract a second glance from anyone seeking an erotic thrill. The plain fact was that, like the vast majority of human beings no longer young, they were a good deal less attractive nude than clothed.

They were an ill-matched pair physically. Peter was a skinny little man with a disproportionately large head and a mass of coarse black hair much like the mane of a horse, which, perched on the top of such a meagre frame, gave a curious impression of top-heaviness. He had a flourishing beard and bad teeth, and he wore silver-rimmed glasses with very thick lenses through which his eyes appeared slightly distorted. There was so little flesh on his chest that the outline of the rib-cage was clearly discernible under its tight covering of skin, and his arms and legs were mere sticks.

Petra, in contrast, was large and plump, with pendulous breasts and folds of loose flesh around her waist and thighs. She had blonde hair plaited into two pigtails and coiled over her ears like a pair of headphones. Equipped with a spear and shield, a helmet and armour, she might have made a passable Valkyrie – if she had had the voice.

Both were in their forties, and as far as Sterne could judge, were perfectly happy in their marriage. They were childless, and perhaps preferred it that way, being quite content with each other's company and desiring no larger family. They had many acquaintances but, so it appeared, no intimate friends. Their surname was Lakos, which was possibly Middle European. They spoke perfectly correct English with a slight foreign accent, and Sterne would have made a guess that they had come to this country to escape from some tyranny or other; possibly fearing the wider spread of Naziism, which was like a cancer at the heart of the Continent and reaching out to other parts.

Sterne had been invited to join the sessions of meditation on various occasions. Indeed, Peter had urged him to do so.

'You would find it mentally refreshing, David. It is a cleansing of the mind, an emptying of all the clutter, so that newer and more profitable thoughts may find a place. For you in your profession it might be especially useful.'

This had been in the early days of his occupation of the flat. He walked out into the garden one afternoon and came upon the landlord and his wife hunkered down on a kind of prayer mat with hands on knees in a rough approximation of the basic yoga posture and without a stitch of clothing between the pair of them.

He muttered an apology and was turning to go when Peter stopped him with a word.

'Wait!'

He halted.

'There is no need to run away,' Petra said. 'You have the freedom of the garden, you know.'

Neither of them appeared to be at all embarrassed by his presence. The embarrassment was all his. He tried not to look directly at Petra, at her heavy breasts and bulging stomach, at the pubic hair, the legs and buttocks squashed beneath her weight.

'Why don't you join us?' she said. Her voice was strangely soft. One might have expected a deep contralto from such a woman, but it was not like that at all. 'Why not take your clothes off too?' She was smiling, as though she found his disconcertion mildly amusing. 'It is so much more comfortable.'

'Oh, I don't think –'

'It is not essential,' Peter said, 'but it is an advantage; a symbolic casting off of the mundane to allow a keener perception of the spiritual. You will be surprised how invigorating it is.'

Sterne decided not to put this assertion to the test. He excused himself and made a hasty retreat to the house. After that experience he had been careful to make sure that no meditation was going on before venturing into the so-called garden.

*

Lakos had a grubby little lock-up shop in a narrow lane not far from Fenchurch Street Station and near enough to the river to catch the odour of mud and rotting timber wafting up whenever the breeze was in the right direction. The shop was side by side with another one where trusses and crutches and artificial limbs and similar orthopaedic devices were sold. Sterne was fascinated and at the same time repelled by the sight of the examples of such goods that were displayed in the window. He wondered whether you could walk in and buy an arm or a leg off the shelf, as it were. The whole thing seemed so improbable, so bizarre; but he had already been long enough in London to be surprised at nothing.

In his shop Lakos appeared to deal mainly in secondhand books. The place was full of them; so full in fact that it was difficult for customers to pass one another in the narrow passages between the shelves. Not that there seemed to be many customers – at least not when Sterne visited the shop; and this made him wonder how Lakos could possibly make a living from the business. Possibly he was in the mail order line.

There was a tiny office at the back, furnished with a couple of chairs and a desk and a safe and a filing cabinet; but nothing gave the impression of much prosperity. Still, there was a saying that where there was muck there was brass; and there was plenty of muck here, if dust and cobwebs qualified for that description.

Lakos appeared delighted to see him on the first occasion when he found his way, not without some little difficulty, to the shop.

'As a man of letters yourself, I am sure you will find much to interest you here.'

No one had ever before called him a man of letters; it sounded rather too grand a description for one in his situation, but he let it pass. Perhaps some day –

A Wind on the Heath

The shop had its own peculiar odour: that smell which old books in the mass exude, mingling with another that might have been dry rot. Rather to his surprise on this occasion Lakos produced a bottle of vodka and a couple of glasses.

'This is a time for celebration, David, my friend. A small drink will do us no harm at all. Come.'

Sterne had no taste for spirits, but it would have seemed churlish to refuse.

Lakos raised his glass. 'To your future. To your brilliant future, David.' He tipped the glass and swallowed the vodka in one gulp.

Sterne felt compelled to follow suit and was conscious of the liquor sliding down his throat and spreading a kind of fire inside him. Would his future be brilliant? He doubted it, but who could tell?

It was at this moment that he became aware of a man standing in the doorway of the office. The man was wearing a black belted raincoat and a black felt hat turned down all round, and he had not spoken a word. But Lakos was disconcerted by his sudden appearance; that much was certain. He took Sterne's empty glass and said:

'You must leave now. Business.' There was a note of urgency in his voice. 'Please go.'

Sterne scarcely had room to squeeze past the man in the doorway. Their faces came close together and their eyes met and locked for an instant. The man's eyes were a steely blue in colour, his unwavering gaze slightly unnerving.

He was never to see the man again and Lakos never mentioned him. There was no reason why he should have done so, of course, but Sterne sensed a mystery. It was a mystery that was to remain unexplained for quite some time to come.

*

When he glanced out of the window again he saw that the meditation was finished. The man and his wife had got to their feet and Peter was rolling up the mat.

The sun had gone behind a cloud and perhaps there was a chill in the air, a hint that summer was passing and autumn was not far away. And after autumn would come winter. For many in Europe it had already come, a man-made frost to chill the blood in the veins. Multitudes would never live to see another spring.

But Peter and Petra Lakos had escaped from that. On this subject they were reticent; he knew nothing of their past. Perhaps it would have been too painful for them to talk about it. He asked no questions, having no desire to pry into something that was really none of his business. One day perhaps they would feel inclined to confide in him, but it was up to them to make the decision. Either way, he was glad that they at least had been able to find refuge before it was too late. They were too nice a couple to be caught up in any purge or pogrom.

He watched them enter the house and it seemed odd to him later, though of course it was not at all odd really, that at that moment he had no intimation whatever of the disaster that was about to occur.

Chapter Two – FIRST RUNG

David Sterne was an East Anglian. He had been born in 1916, the third son of a farmer who cultivated three hundred acres of land close to the border of Norfolk and Suffolk. Like his brothers he had been educated at a boarding school in Bury St Edmunds. Unlike them, he had shown considerable ability as a pupil and also as an athlete. In his final year he had captained the first eleven at cricket and had also won his colours at football.

There had been a suggestion of his going on to Cambridge University, but that had come to nothing. Farming was suffering from the depression and there was not the money to lay out on his further education. He might have gone to work on the farm, but with two brothers older than himself he could see no future in that. He would have been just another hired labourer with nothing to look forward to.

The problem of his future became subject of discussion in the family. Various suggestions were made, some of which from his brothers were merely frivolous, while others did not appeal to him. The fact was that it was a difficult time for job-hunting; millions were on the dole and businesses were going into liquidation everywhere.

His mother thought he should go in for teaching. 'I'm sure you would make a very good teacher, dear,' she said. 'And it's a safe profession. Teachers will always be needed.'

It was a path several of his contemporaries at school had taken, but he had no desire to follow their example. He was quite certain it was not his vocation.

'I'm sorry,' he said, 'but I just don't think I would be a good teacher. I'm not cut out for it.'

She seemed disappointed. 'Are you sure? Why not think about it before you make up your mind?'

'I have thought about it and I know it's not for me. You have to like teaching if you're going to make a job of it.'

'But how do you know you wouldn't like it if you've never tried it?'

'I just do, that's all.'

She sighed. 'Well, if that's the way you feel –'

His father, a thick-set man with a weatherbeaten face and a straggly tobacco-stained moustache, sucked at his pipe and said: 'So if you don't want to be a teacher is there anything you do want to be? Come on, son, let's hear it from you.'

He hesitated. He could guess the kind of reaction there would be if he gave an honest answer. There would be ridicule, laughter, disbelief. They would not understand. They would regard it as sheer stupidity. It would be dismissed as a foolish dream that would never come true.

And perhaps they would be right. Did he himself really believe in the possibility? Perhaps not. Yet he knew that it was what he wanted; there could be no doubt on that point. And so, after the hesitation he said quite calmly:

'I want to be a writer.'

They all stared at him in silence for a moment. Then George and Will burst out laughing. They were much alike, both heavily built young men who took after their father; somewhat ungainly, with a slouching gait and long arms.

He took more from his mother's side of the family. He was lighter, about five feet ten inches in height and sinewy. In fights with his brothers, the sort of fights that boys always have, he would win despite their advantage in size and weight. He was more agile, quicker in his reactions, and quicker-witted too. Not that there had ever been any real enmity between them. The two older boys seemed to accept without ever admitting as much that he was their superior in most ways, and it did not appear to bother them. It was simply in the nature of things. And at least they knew more about farming than he did.

'What you?' George said. 'A writer?'

'You've got to be joking,' Will said. 'You can't be serious.'

'Why not?'

'Well, I mean to say –'

His father sucked at his pipe again, looked hard at him and said: 'Are you serious, Davy?'

He answered with a touch of defiance, as though challenging anyone to doubt it: 'Yes, I am.'

Mr Sterne rubbed his chin. 'Well, I don't know, I'm sure. What makes you think you could make a go of it? What have you written so far?'

'Essays at school. I was pretty good at that. I won prizes for English, you know.'

'Yes, of course. But that's a bit different, isn't it? I mean what we're talking about is being paid for what you do. People don't buy essays, do they?'

'I've written other stuff.'

'What kind of stuff?'

It had been mostly poetry. He had written a lot of poems but he had never shown them to anyone, fearful of ridicule. And he knew there was no money in poetry these days. People seemed to have lost the taste.

So he just said vaguely: 'Oh, this and that.'

His mother said: 'If you were a teacher you could write things in your spare time. The holidays. Teachers have lots of holidays.'

He wished she would not keep harping on that subject. 'I've told you I don't want to be a teacher. And I've written some short stories. One day I'm going to write a novel.'

'Oh my!' Will said. 'Edgar Wallace the Second!'

'Well, it would be nice,' Mrs Sterne said. She was an avid reader of novels when she could spare the time. 'But it must be awfully difficult, don't you think?'

'Of course it's difficult. But other people have done it, so why shouldn't I?'

'You need to have something to write about,' George said. 'What have you got? You don't know anything about life. You're just a kid, not yet dry behind the ears.'

This touched him on the raw, because he knew there was some truth in it. There was of course no possibility of earning a living by his pen at the present time; it was out of the question. Some day perhaps, but not for a long long time; years and years. Meanwhile the urgent need was to find a job of some kind.

*

Unexpectedly, it was his father who came up with a possible solution to the problem a few days later.

'I've been talking to Arthur Martin.'

They were all having supper, which was a meal usually eaten for the sake of convenience seated at the plain deal table in the kitchen. David had never heard of Arthur Martin, but Mr Sterne had made the announcement as though it were of some importance, and there was obviously more to come. He leaned back in his chair and glanced round the table, apparently waiting for some reaction to his words.

No one spoke for a few moments. Then Mrs Sterne said: 'Who is Arthur Martin?'

Mr Sterne gave a lift of the eyebrows, which were bushy and greying. 'You don't know?'

'No, dear, I'm afraid not. Should I?'

'I'm surprised at you.' Mr Sterne shook his head in mock reproof. 'And I am sure Arthur himself would be very disappointed to learn that his name means nothing to some persons in this county. He has rather a good opinion of himself. In fact I sometimes think he believes he's God.'

'Really?'

'Yes, really. And it does amaze me that you can sit there and tell me you've never heard of a man who, in his own estimation at least, has more influence on what the region is thinking than anyone else around.'

'Well, come along then. Don't keep us in suspense any longer. Who is he?'

'Arthur Martin,' Mr Sterne said, 'is editor-in-chief of the *Bury and North Suffolk Morning Post*, commonly known as *The Post*.'

'Oh, the local rag.'

'Local rag, indeed! You'd better not let Arthur hear you call it that. To his way of thinking it's just about on a par with *The Times* and the *Daily Telegraph*.'

'Then he must be the only one who believes that. If he does believe it. Anyway, how do you come to know him?'

'We were at school together. He was pretty brainy but no good at all at games. Always had his nose in a book. Most of us thought he was a bit of a twit really.'

'Oh, I'm sure you would if he didn't like kicking a ball about or swinging a cricket bat. Intelligence would count for nothing against such a handicap. So when did you have this talk with him?'

'Today. When I was in Bury. Thought I might as well take the opportunity while I was there.'

'I don't understand. Why should you want to speak to him? You're not friends, are you?'

'No. But there was a particular reason why I thought it might be a good idea to have a word with him.'

He paused again, smiling, obviously enjoying himself.

Mrs Sterne was obliged to ask the question: 'What reason?'

'Can't you guess?'

'No, I can't. Get on with it.' She sounded impatient.

'Well then, I suppose I'd better tell you. David.'

David was startled. 'Me!'

'Yes, you, boy. You want to be a writer, so I asked Arthur if he'd take you on. Took some persuading, but in the end he agreed to have a look at you. Tomorrow morning you're to go into Bury for an interview. If you make a good enough impression on him you're in.' There was an expression of smug self-satisfaction on the farmer's heavy face as he leaned back in his chair. It was evident that he felt he had brought off quite a coup and ought to be congratulated on it. 'Well? What do you say?'

David hardly knew what to say. He certainly did not feel inflated by this news. His idea of a writer was not someone who worked on a provincial paper like the *Bury and North Suffolk Morning Post*. What he had in mind was an author, a man who had his name on the covers of books, whose stories were printed in magazines, whose productions could be found in public libraries. This which his father was suggesting was a far cry from that.

And why had he not been consulted? It was his life after all. But it was just like the old man to take matters into his own hands without saying a word to anyone. So now this was sprung on him without warning, and no doubt he was expected to jump for joy and offer profuse thanks to the parent who had done so much on his behalf. The trouble was that he did not feel at all grateful. He did not want to go into Bury in the morning; he did not want to see Mr Arthur Martin; above all he did not want to work on the *Bury and North Suffolk Morning Post*.

So he said nothing.

The smugness drifted away from Mr Sterne's features and was replaced by a slight frown.

'Well, I must say you don't look all that happy. Isn't this what you wanted?'

The honest answer to that would have been: 'No, it isn't.' But he lacked the nerve to be quite so blunt. So he said: 'Well, I don't know –'

'Don't know! Damn it, I go out of my way to make this opening for you and you don't know. What sort of an answer is that, for God's sake?'

George gave a laugh. 'You asked for it, Davy; you did ask for it. If you want my opinion –'

Mr Sterne turned on him sharply. 'You can keep your snout out of this. Nobody does want your opinion.'

Mrs Sterne said placatingly: 'It'd be a start for you, Davy dear. You can't expect to be at the top straightaway. This would be the first rung on the ladder, so to speak.'

'Of course it would,' Mr Sterne said. 'You'd be learning the basics. I don't know all that much about this writing business, but I reckon it's a trade like any other, and all trades have to be learnt.'

He felt trapped, and for that he had only himself to blame. He saw that he would have to go along with what his father had arranged for him. There was no way he could avoid this interview that had been fixed for the next morning. And perhaps Mr Martin would reject him anyway. Perhaps he had only agreed to the thing in order to rid himself of the importunate farmer. From what the old man had said, it appeared that he and Arthur Martin had not exactly been bosom chums at school, and there had been little contact between them since those days. So the newspaper editor would hardly have felt compelled to do any favours for his contemporary. All things considered then, the interview was likely to be merely a formality.

Having reached this comforting conclusion he made a show of dropping his reluctance to go along with what had been proposed for his benefit. Nothing would come of it, that was certain. So why worry?

'All right,' he said, 'I'll see Mr Martin. Thanks, Dad.'

No point in antagonising the old man.

Chapter Three – INTERVIEW

The farm was about twelve miles from Bury St Edmunds, where the bones of the martyred King of the East Angles lay beneath the ruins of the ancient abbey. Edmund, captured by the Danes, had stoutly refused to renounce his Christian faith and rule under their supremacy. So he had been stripped naked, bound to a tree and shot at with arrows before being finally beheaded.

David Sterne had been deeply impressed by this story when he first heard it, and often wondered whether he himself would have shown such steadfastness in similar circumstances. Sadly, he had come to the conclusion that he would probably not have done so. He doubted very much whether he was made of the stuff of martyrs. And besides, there already was a Saint David, wasn't there? A Welshman, apparently. To add another to the list could only have led to confusion.

Mr Sterne took him to town in his car, a rather elderly Morris Oxford saloon which he seldom allowed to reach a speed of more than forty miles per hour. He deposited his son outside the rather dingy brick building in a narrow side-street where the publication known as the *Bury and North Suffolk Morning Post* was produced each day.

'I won't come in with you,' he said. 'I've done my bit and now it's up to you.' He gave his son a pat on the shoulder. 'Good luck, my boy.'

David was not sorry that his father was not going in with him. Though he was nervous he preferred to do the talking to Mr Martin without any parental presence. He was wearing his best suit, his shoes were polished and his hair was combed. There was no way he could have made himself more presentable.

There was a reception desk in a kind of lobby where he found himself after passing through the main entrance. A young woman was behind the desk, and she gave him a pleasant smile and asked if she could help him. He could hear mysterious thumpings and other noises coming from other parts of the building and there was a curious odour which he could not identify but thought might be a mingling of paper and printer's ink.

'I have an appointment with Mr Martin,' he said.

'Oh yes.' She seemed to know all about it. 'You'll be Mr Sterne?'

'Yes.'

He thought she was quite attractive in a mature sort of way. He guessed that she must be twenty-five at least.

'He's in his office. I could tell you how to get there, but I think it might be easier if I took you. Don't want you getting lost, do we? Incidentally, I'm Rita Webb.'

She seemed very obliging, but he supposed that was what she was expected to be. He was to learn when he had had more experience of life that women of all ages were inclined to do things for him that they would not have done for everyone; they just looked at him and wanted to help.

'Well, thank you, Miss Webb,' he said. 'It's good of you to take the trouble.'

'No trouble.' She came out from behind the desk. 'This way.'

They came to a flight of bare wooden stairs and she went up in front of him. She was wearing a rather short skirt and a yellow jumper, and as he followed her he could not help noticing that her legs in the sheer silk stockings were a nice shape, a very nice shape indeed. He even reflected that it would have been rather pleasant to touch them, which he could easily have done merely by stretching out his hand, and he wondered what her reaction would have been if he had done so. Shock probably.

But it was no time to be having thoughts about Miss Webb's legs, attractive though they might be. He had to remind himself that he was there for an important interview with Mr Martin and that the silk-clad legs preceding him up the stairs were an irrelevance.

They came to a landing and passed through a large room with a number of desks in it. Some of the desks were occupied, others were not. There were telephones and typewriters on them and there was paper everywhere. There was an air of relaxation about the place; nobody seemed to be doing anything very urgently, though some of the typewriters were clacking. The men were in shirt-sleeves, some talking, almost all smoking.

'This is the newsroom,' Miss Webb said. 'It hots up later. It can get quite hectic when the deadline is approaching.'

Mr Martin's office was at the far end of this room. It had a glass-panelled door with the word, EDITOR, painted on it in black lettering. Miss Webb tapped on the glass with her knuckles, and without waiting for an invitation turned the knob and pushed the door open.

'Mr Sterne to see you, Mr Martin.'

She gave a tug at his sleeve and almost dragged him into the room before retiring and closing the door behind her.

'Well,' Mr Martin said. 'So you're David Sterne.'

'Yes, sir.'

'Your father and I were at school together. But I expect you know that. It was a long time ago. Yes, quite a long time, I'm afraid.'

He was a tall round-shouldered man wearing horn-rimmed glasses. He had what some people called a high forehead, which really meant that he was going bald from the front. His features were thin and there was an ascetic, studious look about him. He had been standing when Sterne was ushered in, but now he sat down behind a desk and invited the younger man to sit down also.

'So,' he said, 'you want to become a newspaperman?'

Sterne wondered what the result would have been if he had replied bluntly that he did not; that it had only been parental urging that had brought him there and that the last thing he really wanted was a job on *The Post*. He decided that it would be unwise to put this to the test, though it would certainly have ensured that he did not get to work on that particular paper. His father would have been certain to hear about it, and that would really have set the sparks flying.

'Well, I thought –' he said, and trailed off, leaving Mr Martin to make what he liked of this.

The editor evidently took it for an affirmative answer. Would the young man have been there otherwise?

'It's an honourable profession; yes, a very honourable one.' He sounded as though he were making a well-rehearsed speech, and it seemed likely that he had made this kind of statement many times before. 'But the work demands certain qualities. Not everyone is equipped – mentally that is – to handle it. Do you think you are?'

Sterne was spared the necessity of making an answer to this question by Martin himself, who went on immediately: 'But of course you do. If you did not I would not be talking to you at this moment.'

It was a curious kind of interview, Sterne thought. Martin did almost all the talking. He seemed to like the sound of his own voice, which was of the fruity variety, and in the course of this one-sided conversation he managed to give a summary of his views on a wide variety of matters. Sterne listened with a show of appreciation and spoke only when directly invited to do so; which was not often. He had no way of telling whether he was making a favourable impression on the editor or not; but he had a feeling that all this was leading up to a final rejection.

The interview was eventually brought to a conclusion when Mr Martin abruptly became transformed from the singular to the plural.

'We will let you know our decision very shortly,' he said, and Sterne gathered that it was not just this person, Arthur Martin, who was speaking now; it was the regal *Bury and North Suffolk Morning Post*.

Miss Webb smiled at him as he passed her desk on the way out.

'Any luck?'

'I'm not sure,' he said. And there was of course the question of what you meant by luck. 'They'll let me know.'

His father asked him a similar question when they met later.

'Did you get the job?'

'They'll let me know. Very shortly.'

*

The letter came two days later in an envelope addressed to Mr David Sterne. It was typewritten on impressively headed writing paper. The paper was white and crisp; it made a crackling sound as he unfolded it. One sentence caught his eye immediately he began to read. It ran:

'We are happy to inform you that your application for employment on this newspaper has been approved.'

There was more – something about a probationary period of engagement etcetera. A salary was also mentioned.

The post had come while the family was at breakfast, and they had all been watching him as he opened the letter. It was obvious to all of them what it was.

'Well, what's it say?' his father demanded.

'They're taking me on.'

His mother was delighted. 'Oh, Davy, I'm so glad.'

'Here,' his father said, 'let me see that letter.'

David handed it to him. Mr Sterne put on a pair of glasses and read it quickly.

'Well, there you are,' he said. 'That's what influence can do for you. He wasn't really looking for anyone, you know; but I persuaded him. The pay's not much though – one pound a week. It's not a lot.'

'It's probably more than he's worth,' George said.

'Now, now, Georgie,' his mother scolded. 'That's not at all a nice thing to say.'

A Wind on the Heath

'But it's probably true all the same,' Mr Sterne said. 'He'll not be much help to them at first. They'll be teaching him.' He peered at his youngest son over the rims of his glasses. 'You're a lucky young man, you know. I hope you realise just how lucky you are.'

'Oh, I do.'

But he did not feel lucky. He had been so sure he would be rejected; he had been counting on it. And now this. Now he would have to go through with it, because there was no way he could pull out after having gone so far; not with everyone thinking it was the best thing that could have happened to him; his father having gone out of his way to help and all that. He regretted now that he had ever mentioned that he wanted to be a writer. That was the kind of thing it was best to keep to yourself. But it was too late to think about that now. The die was cast.

'Well,' his father said, 'I must say you don't sound very enthusiastic. You're not having second thoughts about this, are you?'

'No. Not really.'

'I should think not. This is the sort of opportunity plenty of youngsters would give their ears for. It's an opening for you. No telling where it may lead. It's the beginning. It's the – the –'

'First rung on the ladder?'

'That's it. The first rung, like your mother said.'

Well, perhaps it was at that. But what if it was the wrong ladder?

Chapter Four – LOW KEY

He spent three years on the *Bury and North Suffolk Morning Post*, working his way slowly up that particular ladder. At first he was the lowest of the low, more like an office boy than a newsman. He ran errands, he carried bits of paper here and there, he made tea, and he learned to use a typewriter with two fingers, which was not the way they taught you in the typing schools. He also developed a kind of shorthand of his own which bore little resemblance to the Pitman or any other recognised system.

He was living in Bury, lodging with a widowed aunt who had a Victorian terraced house and a limited income. He propelled himself around on a bicycle at first and went home to the farm at weekends. Later, with the help of a small loan from his father, he bought a secondhand motor-cycle, a 150cc Royal Enfield. This was a boon when he began to be sent round to fêtes and amateur theatrical performances and similar events of less than earth-shaking importance in small towns and villages in the circulation area of *The Post*. Funerals and parish meetings and suchlike were covered by local correspondents – penny-a-liners – who sent in as much copy as possible and had it cut to the bone by the sub-editors.

He joined a tennis club and teamed up with a girl named Phyllis Chambers, who was the daughter of a solicitor. She was a lissome ash-blonde with beautiful legs and a smashing forehand drive. They partnered each other in matches and tournaments and won prizes here and there, playing on soggy vicarage courts and in the gardens of splendid country houses where tea and cakes were handed round between the sets.

For a time he believed he was in love with Phyllis, who had an English rose kind of beauty and the figure of a boy, with no breasts worth mentioning. She came along some time after he had got over his infatuation for Rita Webb, which had always been doomed to end in disillusion, since it transpired that she was engaged to a young man named Cyril Atkins. This individual worked for a firm of insurance brokers and seemed to have a good deal more to offer than David Sterne.

Not that he had ever managed to get at all close to Rita in the spiritual sense. She had always been ready to give him a smile and a friendly word, but she probably had no suspicions that for a time he adored her and dreamed about her and had all sorts of fantasies in which he and she were marooned on desert islands with not another human being in sight. Then one day he met her in the street with this man whom she introduced as Cyril Atkins, her fiancé. After that his feelings for her rapidly cooled, because it seemed ridiculous to be in love with a girl who had such incredibly bad taste as even to think of marrying a stick like this Atkins character. And besides, she was far too old anyway.

It was because of Phyllis Chambers that he got rid of the Royal Enfield. She refused point-blank to ride on the pillion; and in any case it would have been out of the question to travel around on it dressed in tennis clothes and carrying racquets. They were forced to beg lifts from other players who had cars, and this was not at all satisfactory.

'It's so demeaning,' Phyllis said. 'You really ought to have a car, you know. It would be so much more convenient, wouldn't it?'

He had to agree that it would; there could be no question about that. The only problem was how to obtain a car when his finances were already stretched to the limit.

'Everybody has a car these days,' she said. Which was patently untrue of course, but which he saw no point in denying. 'Without a car you're so, well, limited, if you see what I mean.'

'Yes, I do see what you mean.'

'So you will get one, won't you? Because I really don't see how we can go on like this.'

He detected a veiled hint that in the continued absence of a car she might have to think about finding a different partner, and the possibility alarmed him. He did not want to lose her.

'I'll see what I can do,' he said.

She looked pleased. 'I knew you would, David. And it really will make things so much better, won't it?'

*

He appealed to his father again. Unlike Phyllis Chambers, Mr Sterne failed to see the necessity of his son's owning a car.

'What's wrong with the motor-bike?'

'There's nothing wrong with it, but a car would be more convenient in lots of ways.'

Mr Sterne gave him a shrewd look. 'It's that girl, isn't it? You want a car so you can take her about in it.'

'It's not just that. It'd be better for my work. And now that I'm earning more I could pay you back before long. It'll just be a loan, Dad.'

He had already seen the car. It was a Morgan three-wheeler, rather old but in running order. He gave the Royal Enfield in part exchange, and with the loan he had persuaded his father to advance he made himself the owner of something which, although it was powered by a two-cylinder air-cooled engine very plainly visible at the front, was nevertheless undoubtedly a car.

It had its drawbacks. It was noisy, it was smelly, it was far from comfortable to ride in, and the hood was in such poor condition that water tended to leak through whenever it rained. When the weather was warm and the sun was shining it was fine; you felt the breeze in your hair and the exhilaration of speed which was more apparent than real. As the season changed from summer to autumn and then to winter, however, you needed to be well wrapped-up against the chill.

Phyllis was not greatly impressed. 'It's a hybrid, isn't it? It's a kind of mechanical half-breed, neither one thing nor the other. But I suppose it's better than the bike.'

She was nineteen years old and living with her parents in a fairly large house on the outskirts of the town. She was an only child and she had a job in her father's office, though Sterne had a feeling that she did not take this work very seriously. No doubt she would expect to marry eventually and make a home of her own.

He had been introduced to Mr and Mrs Chambers, and he could tell that they did not regard him with much favour. He felt that they looked upon him as something rather distasteful that their daughter had brought into the house. The fact that he worked on *The Post* was obviously not considered to be very much to his credit.

Mr Chambers was a pale sour-looking man and his wife was a fading blonde with rather too much jewellery about her person. In her Sterne might have seen a preview of what Phyllis could be in another thirty years or so. But the thought did not enter his head. He was far too nervous under the probing eyes of the parents of the girl he was currently in love with.

'So you're David Sterne,' Mr Chambers said. He had a rather high-pitched whinnying sort of voice and he made his words sound like an accusation of some misdemeanour. 'Hear you're a journalist.'

Sterne had never yet got round to describing himself as a journalist; it sounded altogether more impressive than reporter. But there seemed to be no need to point out this distinction to the solicitor, so he just said:

'Yes, sir.'

'Future in it, d'you think?'

'I hope so.'

'On that paper?'

'Not necessarily.'

'Ah, so you're thinking of moving on? Up to London, perhaps?'

'It is a possibility, I suppose.'

'You'd be well advised to. Young man like you. Don't want to get yourself bogged down in a backwater like this.'

Sterne could not help feeling that what Mr Chambers had in mind was the idea that his removal to London would take him away from Phyllis and put paid to any liaison between the two that might be raising its ugly head. No doubt he had other plans for his daughter, plans which did not include marriage to someone so completely ineligible as he obviously was.

Mrs Chambers said, with a slight quiver of her chins: 'Phyllis tells me you are a very good tennis player, David.'

'I'm glad she thinks so,' Sterne said.

'Don't you?'

'Oh yes. But I could be biased, couldn't I? She's very good too, of course.'

'So you make an excellent pair?'

The question could have had a double meaning. She might not have been referring solely to tennis. Sterne side-stepped the alternative allusion.

'We win a lot of games.'

He was glad to get away from the house; it had an oppressive effect on him. There seemed to be no real comfort in it. There was a lot of solid furniture, heavy draperies, thick carpets, a lingering odour of floor polish and not a speck of dust anywhere. It was quite unlike his farmhouse home, which had a permanent appearance of untidiness, a lived-in feeling, a welcoming warmth. He preferred that kind of thing.

*

The Morgan made a great different to his life; it widened his range. He was able to take Phyllis to Ipswich and Norwich, where there was more choice of the latest films than in Bury. They went to dances and lent each other books, and though he was always short of money he felt pretty happy, all things considered.

It lasted for about a year. Then she began to cool, started making excuses for not keeping appointments with him, that sort of thing. And one day, when she had told him she had a previous engagement with her parents, he happened to see her riding in a brand-new MG Midget which was being driven by a young man with slicked-back hair, wearing a blue blazer and a spotted silk scarf.

He taxed her with this next day.

'You lied to me.'

'Well, yes,' she admitted, 'I suppose I did fib a little.'

'Who was he?'

'Alan Newcombe. He's my cousin. He's joining Daddy's firm.'

'I see. And now I suppose you prefer his company to mine?'

'You don't understand –'

'Or maybe it's the car. I can see that a new MG Midget would have more attraction than a beat-up old Morgan three-wheeler.' He spoke bitterly, because he felt bitter. 'But I think you might have told me. You might at least have done that.'

'I was going to. I just didn't want to hurt you.'

'That was very considerate of you.'

'Please don't talk like that,' she said. 'I'm sorry; I really am sorry. You have to believe it. But it's all over between us. It has to be. I'm in love with Alan.'

'Ha!' he said. It was not the most intelligent of comments, but he could think of nothing else on the spur of the moment.

'You're angry, aren't you?' she said. 'Yes, I can see you are. But you mustn't be. I mean it's just something that happens.'

'Oh, of course.'

'I didn't mean to fall in love with him. I couldn't help it.'

'Well,' he said, 'so that's that.'

'I'm afraid it is. Sorry, David.'

That was how it ended. Low key. So damned low key.

Chapter Five – FATE

In a way it was a relief. A blow also of course, straight between the eyes. But the blow was temporary; the relief was permanent. Now he would never have to go to that awful house again and try to be polite to those awful parents who made scarcely any effort to conceal the fact that they regarded him as a piece of dirt, quite unfit to be their daughter's boyfriend. They had always wanted to be rid of him and now they were. And he was rid of them, thank God.

Now he could get down to some serious writing; he would have the time. With Phyllis on his hands he had written hardly anything except stuff for *The Post*, which could by no stretch of the imagination have been described as creative writing. Running around with her, he had given barely a thought to anything else. He saw now that he had wasted a whole year; but now with her off his mind he would really get down to it and make up for lost time.

He still played tennis of course, but she was no longer his partner. This worm Alan Newcombe had joined the club and she was paired with him. He always looked immaculate in his pressed white flannels and his Viyella shirt, with never a hair out of place under the controlling application of Brylcreem. His racket was one of the most expensive Wisdens, but Sterne was pleased to observe that he was no great shakes as a player. He was not good enough for his partner in fact, but she was too besotted with him to give him the boot. She no longer won anything, but apparently that was a price she was willing to pay.

He himself had a variety of partners; they were practically queueing up to play with him; which was flattering, to say the least. None of them was as good as Phyllis, and he did not get so involved with them as he had with her, though some of them might have liked him to.

And then another summer was gone and he was able to devote even more of his spare time to that occupation which he had to believe would eventually make his fortune.

He was still writing poetry, but he was turning more and more to the short story, which was likely to be more profitable. There was no shortage of markets; there were monthly magazines galore: *Pearson's*, the *Strand*, the *Red*, the *Blue*, the *Grand, Nash's Pall Mall*, the *Happy*, the *Sunny, Cornhill, Blackwood's, Argosy, Twenty Story*, the *Windsor* and many more. There was a multitude of women's journals and there were weeklies like *John Bull, Tit-Bits, Punch, Answers, London Opinion* and the *Humorist*, all publishing stories. An industrious author could make a decent living from writing nothing else.

He had bought a secondhand L.C. Smith typewriter, and he hammered out his stories on this and sent those he considered the best of them to various publications. They came back with sickening regularity, rejection slips attached to them with paper-clips. Sometimes he felt so discouraged that he thought of packing it in, his faith in himself sadly battered. Was there some vital secret for breaking into the market, a secret he had failed to discover? Many of the stories he read in magazines were no better than those he had written; he was convinced of that. Yet they had got into print and his had not. Why?

His aunt was worried about him. 'You shouldn't stay indoors so much in the evening. It can't be good for a young man like you. You should go out more, enjoy yourself like you used to do with that nice girl. Can't you find somebody else?'

'Easily. But that wouldn't get the writing done.'

'But do you have to write so much, dear?'

'Yes, I do. It's my future, you see.'

He knew that she did not see and that she would continue to worry about him. But it had to be. It was his destiny.

'I'm all right, Auntie. I'm quite all right. Don't bother yourself about me.'

*

He came across an advertisement in *John O'London's Weekly*. It read: 'The Chancery Literary Agency specialises in placing the work of the unknown author. The highest prices are obtained and clients are paid immediately on acceptance of work, without extra charge.'

There was more, but this was enough. It occurred to him that this was what he had been needing all along – an agent. Perhaps editors scarcely glanced at work sent to them by the authors themselves. Perhaps all successful authors had agents. Perhaps this was the key.

He sent one of his best stories to the Chancery Literary Agency and received a prompt reply. The story was good; it deserved publication; but what it needed was a little expert revision to make it saleable. The C.L.A. was ready to undertake this work at the very reasonable fee of three shillings and sixpence per thousand words. They awaited his further instructions.

He felt a trifle disappointed. In his opinion the story had been perfectly all right as it was. But he supposed the C.L.A had had enough experience to know what was what; and if they revised the story it might make them all the more determined to get a sale for it. So, after some reflection, he decided to send a postal order for half a guinea to cover the cost of revising his three thousand word story.

The revised version arrived a week later. The blue pencil had been freely wielded and he was aghast to see the mayhem that had been inflicted on his story. Quite frankly he did not see how it was any better than it had been before; in fact he would have said it was worse. But he typed it out again with the changes that had been made and sent it back to the agency, together with the fee of another half-guinea which had been demanded to cover the expense of submitting it to as many markets as would prove necessary before the almost certain sale had been obtained.

There followed a long long silence from the C.L.A. After three months had elapsed he wrote to the agency inquiring whether they had yet had any success with the story. By return of post the manuscript came back with a list of magazines to which it had apparently been submitted. There was also a letter. The C.L.A. regretted that they had had no success in placing this particular story, but he would of course appreciate the fact that there were many reasons why a certain story might prove unacceptable at any given time. However, if he had other stories he would like them to handle for him they would be only too pleased to do so, provided the work was up to standard. They looked forward to hearing from him in due course.

He decided to have no further dealings with them, but to set down the whole sorry business as experience. He was to learn that there were a lot of sharks swimming around in the murky waters of the publishing world, eagerly snapping at any morsel that might come within reach. He had been bitten by one of them, but he would not let it happen again. There were firms eager to publish your novel if you paid them for the privilege. They were known as vanity publishers, and they did very little in the way of selling the books they produced. For his money the gullible author ended up with a pile of volumes which no one would buy, and he could either store them in the attic or give them away to friends and acquaintants.

*

Having been disillusioned by his dealings with the Chancery Literary Agency, Sterne came to the conclusion that an agent was not the magic key to success as an author and that the only way was to persevere with his own efforts to surmount the intangible barrier that seemed to exist between his stories and the printed page. And after a time he had some crumbs of encouragement. Now and then, instead of the printed rejection slip he would receive a brief note from the editor telling him that a story of his had almost made it and that other products of his pen would be welcomed for consideration. Spurred on by these magical words, he would hammer out more and more material on the old L.C. Smith and post it off to various destinations. But still it all came back, as though each manuscript had been a homing pigeon bound to return to the place from which it had come.

It seemed hopeless. There were days when he would despair, would call himself a fool for entertaining such ridiculous impossible dreams. Why not face the unpalatable truth that he simply did not have it in him to make the grade? He might as well make one big pile of all his stories so laboriously typed out in double spacing on quarto paper and set a match to it. He would be free then; free of this hope that was nothing but a mockery.

But those days passed and he refused to give up. He had to have faith in himself, had to believe that if he continued pushing at the door it would finally open and he would be admitted to that paradise inhabited by the published author. One day it would happen.

And one day it did. There was a letter in a small white envelope instead of a rejected manuscript in a large buff one.

It was a letter of acceptance from the *Happy Magazine*. The editor liked his story, *Where the Sun Shines*, and had pleasure in offering three guineas for First British Serial Rights.

For a moment he felt quite giddy with elation and the print danced before his eyes. It was the breakthrough he had been seeking. Suddenly the door was open and from this point the going would be easy. At least, that was what he told himself.

He was wrong. The fact that one story had found favour in the eyes of one editor did not mean that all the others would henceforth be falling over one another to get hold of his work. There was still a long way to go, still many disappointments ahead; but just for now he was in ecstasy, and he felt that even in these depths of winter the sun was shining warmly for him.

The first person he told was his aunt. She was very pleased for his sake.

'I'm sure it's only what you deserve, dear. After all that hard work you've put in.'

She had never read anything of his and he doubted whether she had even heard of the *Happy Magazine*. He thought she might have shown a little more enthusiasm; she was taking it very calmly. But he supposed it would have been foolish to expect anything more demonstrative from her. She could have no conception of the truly earth-shaking impact of this event.

Rita Webb was more impressed when he told her. She was still Miss Webb, though still engaged to Cyril Atkins, who seemed to be in no hurry to buy the wedding ring.

'Oh, it's wonderful, David,' she said. 'I'm so glad, I really am. I mean it's such an achievement, isn't it? Quite a feather in your cap. I'm sure there'll be some people round here who'll be envious.'

'Well,' he said, 'it's really not much, you know.' Playing it down, being falsely modest when all the time he knew it was a great deal, a tremendous thing, a dream come true.

'Oh but it is, it is,' she said. Which was of course what he wanted her to say. 'You're going to make it, David; I know you are.'

'I just hope you're right,' he said.

*

Mr Martin got to hear about it, as he was bound to do. Miss Webb had not kept the news to herself, and everyone on the paper soon knew about this small success of his as a fiction writer. He was summoned to the editor's office where Mr Martin tackled him on the subject.

'What's this I hear about you writing short stories and selling them to magazines?'

'Not them,' Sterne said. 'So far I've only sold one.'

'Well, that's the way it starts, isn't it? First the one, then others. Wouldn't you say so?'

'It's what I'm hoping of course. But I'm not counting on it.'

This was not strictly true. He was convinced now that he had found the way in with one story a flood of them would surely follow where this had led.

'Oh,' Martin said, 'I'm sure it will happen. And I fear we shall soon be losing you. A young man of your literary ability will not be content to linger in these backwoods. You are obviously destined for higher things.'

Sterne detected a note of sarcasm and had the odd impression that the editor was jealous. Could it be that he had once nourished ambitions of a similar nature? Ambitions that had never come to fruition and were never likely to do so now. Was the summit of his career to be nothing more elevated than editorship of an obscure provincial newspaper?

It was obvious that any congratulations which might be forthcoming from the man were likely to be extremely muted, but he refused to let this discourage him. What Martin had suggested with faint mockery, that he might soon be leaving *The Post*, coincided with what he had in his own mind. It would not, of course, happen immediately; for the present he had to hang on here because there was no other way he could make a living. But eventually he would go. London beckoned, and it was to that Metropolis he must, like Dick Whittington, make his way in search of fame and fortune.

*

He told no one at the office the size of the fee which was being paid for the story; it was hardly large enough to sound impressive. Let them imagine if they would a much higher figure. As perhaps the next one might be.

But the next one was a while in coming. He had to wait nearly six months for it. And then two more came in quick succession, and he began to think he might soon be able to make the move away from *The Post* that was always in his mind.

Still, a handful of short story sales was hardly a solid enough basis on which to make such a decision. With no more than this flimsy encouragement it would have been folly to take such an important step. He had reluctantly to accept the likelihood of having to remain in his present situation for quite a few more years to come.

He had not, however, foreseen that fate might take a hand in the game. But it was fate, chance, destiny, fortune, call it what you might, that was to make possible what had seemed impossible and open up the way ahead.

He won a prize in a football pool.

Chapter Six – BREAK

It was not one of the really big prizes, which could run into thousands and tens of thousands. It was in fact exactly eight hundred and seventy pounds five shillings and sixpence.

Not a fortune. No, not by any means a fortune. But it was enough perhaps; enough to bring about a most remarkable alteration in his way of life and to set him on the path that was to lead to experiences such as he would never have imagined even in the wildest flights of fancy.

He did not need to spend a moment in reflection; he knew at once that this was his chance and he had to seize it. Not to do so would have been to make the admission that he had no faith in his own ability, his own talent; that he was resigned to nothing better than a slow ascent of the ladder of provincial journalism. He would not, he could not submit himself to that when he had been offered this lifeline to better things.

He announced his decision to the family when they were all at supper in the farmhouse kitchen the next weekend.

'I am going to London.'

It caused no immediate stir. They did not grasp at once the full import of the statement.

His mother said: 'That will be nice for you, dear. Will it be for the paper?'

'No,' he said. 'I'm leaving *The Post*. I've handed in my resignation.'

This brought a reaction. They all stared at him. Mr Sterne put down his knife and fork. They made a faint clatter as they hit the plate.

'Are you out of your mind?'

'I don't think so.'

'But you're leaving *The Post*?'

'Yes.'

'And going off to London?'

'Yes.'

'For how long?'

'I don't know. For as long as it takes, I suppose.'

'What does that mean, for God's sake?'

George gave a laugh. 'He means as long as it takes him to make his fortune. It's the pools win that's done it. It's gone to his head.'

He had felt compelled to tell them about that, and they had all said how lucky he was. George and Will had found it difficult to conceal their envy. It was money for nothing, and they had never had anything like it; they had to slave away on the farm for anything the old man could be persuaded to pay them. Which was not a lot. They had to be content with assurances that it would all be theirs when he died. Since he looked the picture of rude health and vitality, the prospect appeared far too distant to give much consolation.

'Eight hundred pounds isn't going to last long in London,' Mr Sterne said. 'You'll soon run through that.'

'Then he'll come back here begging for help,' Will said. 'It's just plain crazy. Money down the drain.'

'It's my money,' David said. 'I can do what I like with it.'

'But Davy,' his mother said, 'who'll look after you?'

He smiled at her reassuringly. 'I can look after myself. I'm not helpless, you know.'

'But you're so young.'

'I'm nearly twenty-one. I'll manage.'

'I suppose,' his father said, 'you're reckoning on making a living with that writing of yours. Is that it?'

'I'm going to try. I may get a job on a newspaper.'

Arthur Martin had promised to give him a favourable reference. He had become quite affable now that he knew Sterne was leaving.

'We shall miss you. But it's probably for the best. You have talent and I'm sure you'll make the grade. And of course I shall always be happy to consider any little pieces of yours that you feel might fit into our columns.'

'Thank you, sir,' Sterne said. 'I'll remember that.'

Miss Webb gave him a parting kiss and wished him the best of luck. 'I remember the day you came here, David. Seems like yesterday.'

'It was three years ago.'

'As long as that! How time flies! Well, don't forget us.'

He promised not to.

He thought of paying a call on Phyllis Chambers to say goodbye. And then he thought better of it. They had split up long ago and he had no desire to go to that awful house and maybe see those awful parents again. Better to leave well alone.

*

There were tears running down his mother's cheeks when he was leaving. She hugged him as though reluctant to let him go.

'You will take care of yourself, won't you?'

He said he would.

'And don't forget to write.'

He might have told her that writing was the main object of the exercise, but he knew what she meant: letters home.

He promised not to forget.

His father took him to the railway station at Bury in the car. The farmer had come to accept with resignation this venture which he still regarded as extremely rash and almost bound to end in disillusion if not complete disaster. He offered his work-roughened hand in farewell and David clasped it.

'Goodbye, Dad.'

'Goodbye, Davy. And remember, whatever happens, we're backing you.'

He watched from the carriage window as the train pulled out. He watched until the figure of his father dwindled and finally disappeared from view. Then he took his seat and sat there, listening to the clatter of the wheels on the rails as the train gathered speed and feeling excitement bubbling up inside him. He had made the break; he was going to a new life; heading into the unknown. There was a trace of apprehension mixed in with the excitement and the delight. He was on his own now, with no one to help him. He had to do it all for himself.

He listened to the drumming of the wheels and thought of that great city coming nearer and nearer. London; the very name had magic in it. It was a city of dreams. He hoped and had to believe that it was the city where his own dreams would come true.

When he stepped out of the carriage into the echoing smoky cavern that was Liverpool Street Station he thought: 'This is it. This is where it all begins. This is the gateway.'

There were crowds of people leaving the train; they came bursting out of it like a torrent of water suddenly released by the opening of the floodgates. Luggage in hand, he went along with the stream. There were porters pushing barrows loaded with trunks and suitcases, and there was a rank of taxicabs to the left. But he used neither taxi nor porter; they were luxuries reserved for people with more money than he had to spare.

*

He found temporary accommodation at a YMCA hostel. The room was small, little more than a cubicle. He knew that he could not work in such a place and he regarded it simply as a base from which he could carry out a search for more suitable quarters.

It took him a week to find what he was looking for. He saw the advertisement in an evening paper: 'Furnished flat to let. One bed. Bath. Reasonable rent. Suit single gentleman or young couple.'

The address was in the Islington area, and there was an Underground station within easy walking distance. He could not have asked for any more convenient situation. The advertisement did not state that it would suit a writer, but he felt that it might well do so.

He arrived in the afternoon. He discovered that the house was in the middle of a terrace and faced on to a rather unimpressive street with a row of dingy-looking trees planted along one side. All the houses had tiny front gardens, which were enclosed by low brick walls and wrought-iron gates. Most of the gardens consisted of nothing more than a patch of rough grass passing as a lawn and a short paved path leading up to the front door. It was the kind of neighbourhood where the residents tended to keep themselves to themselves and had no inclination to pry into one another's business. Lower middle class English to the core.

And yet the woman who came to the door of Number 23 in answer to his ringing of the bell spoke with a foreign accent.

'I have come,' Sterne said, 'about the advertisement of a furnished flat.'

'Ah yes.' The woman gave him a quick appraising look and seemed to come to the conclusion that there was nothing about his appearance to give her any doubts regarding him. 'You wish to see the flat?'

He saw that she was rather large and plump and middle-aged, and the best that could be said for her features was that they were homely. She was blonde and there was a mole on the left side of her upper lip. She was wearing a long black dress which looked as if she might have made it herself; it was like a sack with sleeves.

'If it would not be too much trouble.'

'No trouble at all,' she said. 'Please to come inside.'

She held the door open for him and he walked past her into the narrow entrance hall. She closed the door, taking some of the light from the hall, which with dark brown paint on the walls tended to be somewhat gloomy.

'It is upstairs,' she said. 'And now I should tell you that my name is Petra Lakos. Mrs Lakos.'

'I am David Sterne.'

'Good,' she said, as though giving her approval of the name. 'Now we will go up the stairs and you will look at the flat.'

She led the way and he followed. They came to a landing and she opened a door which gave access to a fair-sized room rather sparely furnished with a table, chairs and a sideboard, all of which looked like pieces picked up in a sale; much-used but adequate for their purpose. On one side was a sofa with a scattering of cushions.

'Our previous tenant,' Mrs Lakos said, 'was a student. Such a nice boy. He completed his studies and left. Are you a student, Mr Sterne?'

'No,' he said. And then after a moment's hesitation: 'I'm a writer.'

It seemed to impress her, which made him feel rather guilty, though it was after all the truth.

'A writer! Oh, how splendid! I am sure you will find this flat to suit you very well. It is a quiet area and you will not be disturbed. And my husband, he is also, as you might say, a literary man.'

'He is?'

'Oh yes. He sells books, you know. Old books.'

'I see.'

So if he took the flat he would have for a landlord a dealer in secondhand books. He wondered whether this would be a good thing or a bad, and came to the conclusion that it made no difference either way.

And the flat appeared suitable. It was certainly not luxurious, but he was not looking for luxury; low rental was the prime consideration, and the figure that Mrs Lakos mentioned seemed very reasonable; it would not cut too deeply into his limited capital, and of course he would be hoping to earn something from his writing to augment it. If that failed, all failed. But he must not think of failure. He had to succeed.

The bedroom was not large, but it accommodated a double-bed, a dressing-table and a wardrobe without too much cramping. The bath was small, but it needed to be in order to fit into the bathroom. There was a kitchenette with a sink and a gas cooker. All in all it would suit him very well.

'You like it?' Mrs Lakos asked.

'Yes,' he said. 'I'll take it.'

'I shall have to consult my husband of course. But I am sure he will approve. He should be home soon. If you would like to wait?'

Sterne said he would.

Mrs Lakos offered to make tea, and they drank it together in the ground-floor sitting-room, which was larger and a good deal more cluttered than the one above. She produced a fruit cake too, and cut a generous slice for the prospective tenant. He was still eating it when Mr Lakos walked in.

Mrs Lakos made the introduction. 'Mr Sterne, my dear. A writer. Wishes to take the flat. What do you think of that?'

Lakos did not say what he thought of it. He gave Sterne a close inspection, peering at him through his silver-rimmed glasses as if at a piece of merchandise of doubtful quality which he had been invited to buy. Then he said abruptly:

'What do you write?'

'Short stories, newspaper articles, that kind of thing.'

'And you sell them?'

'Some of them. I'm hoping eventually to write a novel.'

'Ah! It is a hope that rather a lot of people have, I believe. And you wish to rent the flat?'

'Yes.'

'Very well,' Lakos said. 'Very well.'

It was as simple as that. No references demanded; no formalities of any kind. A brief inspection of the applicant was apparently enough for the Lakoses. They liked the look of him, and that was that.

He returned to the YMCA hostel to fetch his luggage and moved into Number 23, Rosetta Avenue.

Chapter Seven – HOBBY

It was not from that time forward a tale of ever-increasing success. Far from it. Sales came by fits and starts. He wrote industriously, producing an impressive volume of work, but only a disappointingly small proportion of it ever got into print. He was certainly not making a living from the old L.C. Smith, and he had to draw regularly from his capital to see him through.

Yet he did not lose heart. He could go on like this for a long time yet; for he lived frugally and had no heavy expenses. Gradually the gap between income and expenditure must surely narrow until eventually the former came to exceed the latter. This at least was what he told himself.

The Lakoses were constantly encouraging. They rejoiced in his successes and commiserated with him on his failures. It sometimes seemed to him that they were as eager for him to succeed as he was himself, and he was quite sure that it was not because of any fear that he might default on the rent of the flat if his earnings did not come up to scratch. He was convinced that their concern for his welfare was motivated by nothing else but a regard for him as a person. They liked him and he liked them in return, though he could not deny the fact that they were an odd couple.

There was a certain mystery about them too, which intrigued him. He had fantasies about them and toyed with the idea of weaving a story around the pair. But this never came to anything.

He did soon learn one thing about Petra. Indeed, it would have been difficult to make a secret of it, and she made no attempt to do so. She was a medium. She held séances in the sitting-room on the ground floor, and occasionally he would be invited to join in – just to make up the number. He was perfectly willing to oblige, regarding it as the kind of experience which might be used as material in some future work of fiction. Grist to the mill in fact.

It was all rather eerie. The heavy curtains would be drawn if the séance was taking place during the day, so that everything took place in partial darkness, a gloom in which the various participants could be only dimly seen. There would usually be half a dozen or so, and they would sit round a circular table and link hands. There would be a curious scent in the room, which was produced by Mrs Lakos burning what might have been a kind of joss-stick before the proceedings began. It was rather like incense, and he was not sure whether this was supposed to serve as an aid to the supernatural or whether it was designed merely to counteract the none too pleasant odour given off by the bodies and clothing of some of the people in the room. These were chiefly middle-aged women, though now and then there would be a man who wished to make contact with someone in what Mrs Lakos called 'the other world'.

When the group had been fitted into place round the table and had joined hands there would often be strange noises such as knocking or rustling or sibilant whispering, and possibly the table would move. Eventually Mrs Lakos would lie back in her chair, give a deep sigh and go into a trance, eyes closed and quite motionless. Then after a time if things were going well she would make contact with one of her spirit guides. There were two of these: one was an Indian chief named Running Deer and the other was a young girl named Sylvia. Apparently these guides had dealings with a whole raft of characters who had passed over, and the curious thing was, to Sterne's way of thinking, that so many of these people just happened to be the deceased relatives or friends of one or other of the persons seated round the table.

It was the job of Running Deer and Sylvia to transmit messages from the other world through Mrs Lakos, and the words that came from her mouth while she was in the trance were spoken in quite different accents from her normal voice: one was gruff and manly while the other was high-pitched and childlike. Whichever of these voices was on duty at the moment would hold a question-and-answer dialogue with one of the persons at the table, acting as a link with somebody at the other end of the line who might be identified as Uncle Henry or Cousin Ellen or maybe poor little Cathie who had died young.

What impressed Sterne about all this was the triviality of the subjects under discussion. The information coming through from that world over there was pretty mundane to say the least. What he would really have liked to hear was just how they had got there, what sort of travelling arrangements had been made for them and what kind of place they were living in now. A few details of that sort: descriptions of architecture, food, entertainment, scenery and so on would have been really interesting. But nothing like this ever passed across the great divide; it was as if these people were just floating in space, in a vast emptiness, with nothing occupying their minds but the same old worthless trash that had been in them when they lived on earth. It was all a great disappointment; there should have been more to it than this.

But of course it was just a farce, an act put on by Mrs Lakos. There was no doubt that she did it very well. She hoodwinked the gullible people who came to the séances and paid her for the privilege of being led up the garden path. And was there any harm in it? They got what they came for: apparent contact with a departed loved one, reassurance that there was life after death, a cosy little get-together with others of like minds, and tea and cakes to round off the proceedings. They went away feeling the better for it, and what more could one ask for?

He had a suspicion that Peter helped with the special effects. He would be at home but was never visible at the séance, though he might have been hiding behind a screen or maybe in an adjoining room. The effects could be quite spectacular at times: trumpets floating in mid-air and emitting brazen notes, ectoplasm apparently emanating from the unconscious medium, ghostly figures drifting around and so on.

He never suggested to either of the Lakoses that the séances might be faked. He had no wish to offend them. But he suspected that they might have doubts about his belief in the authenticity of the proceedings, though they did not say so. It was as if there were a tacit agreement to regard as genuine what they all knew to be nothing but a charade.

*

His suspicion that Peter had a hand in these performances was strengthened by something that happened not long after his taking residence in the flat. He had bought a secondhand wireless set, a Cossor, and within a few days it had broken down. He told Lakos, bemoaning the fact that it was money down the drain.

'Let me have a look at it,' Lakos said.

He failed to see what good that would do, but it could do no harm, so he agreed. They went up to the flat and Lakos took the back off the set. He seemed to know what he was doing and after a brief inspection he said:

'I cannot test it properly here. But if you like I will have a go at it.'

'But do you know anything about wireless?' Sterne asked. It hardly seemed the kind of knowledge a dealer in secondhand books would possess.

Lakos gave a faint smile. 'A little.'

'Well, if you really think –' Sterne was still doubtful.

'Come,' Lakos said. 'What have you got to lose? Let me take it to my workroom and I will see what I can do.'

It was the first Sterne had heard of any workroom. He said; 'All right, but let me carry it for you.'

'That will not be necessary. It is not heavy.'

He picked up the set and carried it to the door, which Sterne opened for him, expecting him to go down the stairs. But to his surprise Lakos walked to the end of the landing where another staircase led to an attic at the top of the house. He began to climb this, and Sterne was about to follow him but was stopped by a word.

'Don't come up. I can manage quite well.'

Sterne had never been up to that part of the house; it did not go with the flat, which was confined to the one floor. He gathered that Lakos did not want him to see the workroom for some reason or other, though he could not imagine why. Still, if that was his wish he was perfectly entitled to maintain the privacy of the attic. It belonged to him.

*

Chancing to encounter him in the hallway the next day, Sterne asked him how he was getting on with the set.

'I have found the trouble,' Lakos said. 'It is one of the valves. I know a place where I can get a replacement cheap. Do you wish me to?'

'Why, yes,' Sterne said. 'That would be fine.'

*

He saw nothing of Lakos for the next three days and missed having the set. There were some good comedy acts on the BBC which he enjoyed listening to: Stainless Stephen, Rob Wilton, Tommy Handley and Ronald Frankau in their quickfire act as Mr Murgatroyd and Mr Winterbottom, and the incomparable Sage of Hogsnorton, Gillie Potter. With so much happening in Europe, he liked to hear the news bulletins too. Things were looking bad over there and he feared that before long Britain might be dragged into another war. If that happened how would it affect him? He would be involved, that was certain. All things considered, the future looked remarkably dicey.

He decided to go up to the attic and see whether Lakos was there. It was evening and it seemed likely that he would be home from the bookshop by that time; though his movements were unpredictable.

There was no one on the landing when he stepped out of the flat, and he could hear no sound of movement coming from the floor below; so he made his way to the stairs that led upward to another smaller landing and the attic door. This was closed and he tapped on it lightly with his knuckles. There was no response, and after waiting a few moments he turned the knob and discovered that the door was not locked. He pushed it open and took a step into the room and saw that Lakos was indeed there.

The bookseller was seated at a bench which was littered with radio equipment. He had apparently been working on some piece of apparatus and had not heard the light tap on the door. But he had heard it open and it seemed to have given him a shock. He stood up quickly, pushing the chair away, and there was a momentary expression of annoyance on his face when he saw the intruder. But the frown quickly vanished and he spoke quite affably.

'Ah, David, it is you. You have come for your set?'

Sterne could see the Cossor standing on the bench with the other gear, but it was not what Lakos had been working on just then.

'If it's ready. I'm sorry to have disturbed you. I did knock, but I expect you didn't hear me.'

'No matter, no matter,' Lakos said. 'You have discovered my little secret. But it is not of importance. As you see, I dabble in this sort of thing. It is my hobby.'

There was a lot of other paraphernalia filling up much of the space in the attic, and Sterne guessed that some of this might well have been used to produce the supernatural effects for Petra's séances. But he would not have dreamed of suggesting this to Peter.

'And the set?'

'Ah yes, the set. It is once more in going order. I should have returned it to you, but I overlooked it. The new valve cost five-and-six. That is little more than half the amount you would have had to pay for a Marconi or a Mullard or a Mazda. It is a Tungsram, made in Hungary, and is just as good.'

'And I must pay you for your work too.'

Lakos brushed this suggestion aside. 'Oh no, no. I am most happy to help. As I told you, it is my hobby.'

He insisted on going down with Sterne to return the set to its place in the flat and demonstrate that it was now working perfectly again. When it was switched on there happened to be a news bulletin coming through. It included the report of another speech that Hitler had made at a Nazi rally, and a snatch of that ranting voice recorded at the event came bursting into the room with all its menace and suggestion of paranoia.

The effect on Lakos was instantaneous. An expression of horror and loathing contorted his features; small beads of sweat appeared on his forehead; his eyes behind the glasses seemed to bulge and his hands shook.

'That man!' he cried. 'That monster! That maniac!'

He turned abruptly and left the room.

Chapter Eight – DANCING-GIRL

David Sterne saw Angela Street for the first time when she was dancing on the stage of the Windmill Theatre, and from that moment he could not get her out of his mind.

The Windmill did a non-stop revue called Revudeville. You could go in at any time after the doors opened and stay as long as you wished. The show included fan-dancers and specialty-dancers and sketches and conjurors and dramatic monologues and stand-up comedians who had a hard time competing with the scantily-clad dancing-girls. It was a good training ground for them, however, and several progressed from there to higher things.

Sterne did not often go to the Windmill; he could not afford it. In fact, when he first saw Angela Street it was only his second visit, and it was not until later that he learned her name. But he knew at once that he had to speak to her and try to get to know her. He might not be successful, but for his peace of mind he had to make the attempt.

He stayed in his seat until the end of the show and then went round to the stage-door to wait for her to come out. He did not have to wait long. Wearing a white trench-coat and a red beret, she looked very much altered from the girl he had seen on the stage kicking her legs in the air, but he had no difficulty in recognising her. He moved towards her so that he was standing directly in her path.

'Excuse me,' he said.

She scarcely glanced at him. 'No,' she said. 'Excuse me.' She did a neat side-step, brushed past him and went on her way.

She was walking quite quickly, her heels clicking on the pavement. He would have had to run to catch up with her, but he lacked the nerve and a few moments later she was out of sight.

'Damn!' he said. 'Damn and blast it!'

*

He was in the same place at the same time the next night, though he had not been to the show. But she did not emerge with the other performers and again he was disappointed. He was to learn later that there were two companies of dancers – A and B. When A Company was on duty B Company had the day off, and vice versa. If he had been in the theatre he would have known that she had not been on stage that night.

However, he refused to abandon his purpose, and the next evening he was at the stage-door for the third time in as many days. This time he again placed himself in her path, but before she had a chance to brush past he said:

'Do you want some free publicity?'

She told him afterwards that it was the unexpectedness of the question that halted her in her tracks and stopped her from giving him the brush-off again. In his favour there was also the fact that he was not wearing a dirty raincoat.

She peered into his face and said: 'It was you the other night, wasn't it?'

'Yes, it was.'

'So what's all this about free publicity? I don't get it.'

'I thought I might do a feature about you for a newspaper or a magazine.'

'Are you a journalist then?'

'Well, yes, you could say that.'

'You don't seem very sure about it.'

She sounded a trifle suspicious. She was not wearing the beret this time and her black hair was cut in a page-boy style, framing an impish sort of face in which a pair of dark lustrous eyes were set rather widely apart. It had enchanted him when he had seen it at a distance in the theatre, and at close quarters it lost none of its charm. She was young enough for that.

'What I mean is I'm a free-lance. I used to be on a daily paper, but I left to work on my own.'

He did not tell her that it was an obscure provincial paper. If she jumped to the conclusion that he was talking about one of the national dailies, so be it.

'You're not having me on, are you? Just shooting a line. Trying to make me think you're a big shot or something.'

He gave an emphatic denial. 'Oh no; I'm not a big shot. I wouldn't want you to get that idea.'

She gave a laugh, which was a pleasure to hear. 'I wouldn't anyway. I can see you're not.'

He was not sure whether this could be taken as a compliment or quite the opposite. But as if to reassure him and take any sting out of the words she added:

'I mean you're too young, aren't you? Big shots tend to be older and bloated. People I wouldn't give the time of day to.'

'So how does the idea strike you?'

'I don't know.' She seemed undecided. But she was not rejecting the suggestion out of hand, as he had feared she might. 'I'd have to think about it.'

'That's all right. You don't have to make your mind up straightaway.'

She was still looking at him thoughtfully, as though weighing him up in her mind.

'Why me?' she asked.

'How do you mean?'

'I mean there are plenty of other girls in this line of business, so why pick on me? Why not one of the others?'

He decided to be honest. 'I liked the look of you.'

'When you saw me on stage?'

'Yes.'

'I think you're crazy.'

'Maybe I am.' He might have added: 'Crazy about you.' But he did not.

'Look,' she said, 'I have to go. But I'm not working tomorrow. Suppose we meet somewhere and talk about this thing.'

He could not have asked for anything better. He had to restrain himself from giving a whoop of delight; but he kept his voice under control and answered calmly:

'That sounds like a very good idea. Where should we meet?'

She thought about it for a few moments and then suggested Trafalgar Square at midday. He agreed immediately.

'Now I must fly,' she said.

She set off in the direction of Tottenham Court Road, leaving him in a state that was close to delirium. It was not until later that it occurred to him that they had not exchanged names. He still did not know who she was.

*

They had lunch in a Lyons teashop, waited on by a Nippie who appeared to be as young as Angela but not nearly as lovely. He knew her name now and she knew his.

'Angela,' he said, trying it on his tongue. 'That's a nice name. Angela Street. Yes, I like it.'

'Well,' she said, 'what's in a name?' But she seemed pleased. Also, he thought, faintly amused; as though she might have been laughing at him, or perhaps at some secret that she was keeping to herself.

She did not give her story while they were having the meal; it was hardly the right place for confidences of that sort; there were too many people around, too much distraction. When they left the teashop it had begun to rain lightly. The National Gallery presented a refuge from the weather and they took shelter inside. Neither of them was much interested in the pictures at that time, and as they sat side by side on one of the seats she gave a somewhat disjointed account of how she had come to be a dancer at the Windmill Theatre.

Sterne jotted down what she told him in a notebook. He would gather the threads together later and make a product that would, he hoped, be of interest to the average reader. And he soon realised that there were some unusual aspects to the story. For one thing, her origins were not quite what he would have expected.

In the first place it transpired that she was the daughter of a Yorkshire parson. She had been brought up in a remote stone vicarage in bleak Brontë country. Her mother was dead and her father had disowned her when she had run away with a travelling concert party which performed in small towns and villages. By her account it had been a hand-to-mouth existence. She was fourteen at the time of her escape from the vicarage, and it seemed that her father had just let her go; perhaps only too glad to be rid of someone who was only a bother to him. Certainly he had made no effort to bring her back.

The manager of this concert party, which went by the name of The Streamers, became a second father to her. With them she learned to dance and sing and act a bit, and before long she was one of the most valuable members of the troupe. But the time came when Arnold Rankin, the manager, suggested that for her own good she ought to go to London and try her fortune there. Because, although he would be sorry to lose her, it was an unfortunate fact that the day of the travelling concert party was drawing to a close and there was no future in it for her. With her talent she could go on to the very top.

She gave a wry smile when she told him this. 'The very top! The Windmill chorus line! That's a laugh. Though it was enough of a struggle to get even that far. You'll never believe what I've been through.'

Nevertheless, she proceeded to tell him. And it really was quite a story. There were pauses now and then as she seemed to be searching her memory for incidents that might be interesting. There was no chronological order, and he could see that he would have to do a lot of sorting out and rearranging to make a finished job of it. And he would never be able to get it all in; he would just have to pick out the highlights. Already he had a title in his mind: 'Yorkshire Vicarage to Windmill Theatre'.

'Do you think you'll make a go of this?' she asked.

'I hope so. And I don't see why not. It's the sort of story that should have a pretty wide interest. It's got the human touch. I shall need some photographs to go with it, of course.'

She said this was no problem; she had plenty. She promised to bring a selection for him to look at.

'It'll have to be the day after tomorrow. Same place, same time?'

'That'll be fine,' he said.

Chapter Nine – THE PUSH

He had made a first draft of the article, and he brought a copy for her to read when they met again.

'It's only a rough outline,' he said. 'I'll probably have to make a few cuts, because it's rather long. And it could do with some tightening up and re-writing here and there. But read it and see what you think.'

They were in the National Gallery again. There was a Rubens dead in front of them: lots of plump female flesh with a rustic setting; but they had no interest in the painting.

She read the typescript while he examined the photographs she had brought. They were professional jobs and it was going to be difficult to choose the best; they were all good. She was nothing if not photogenic.

She finished reading and looked at him.

'What do you think of it?' he asked.

She said: 'You're pretty good at this sort of thing, aren't you?'

'You think so?'

'Oh yes. It's easy to read. It goes very smoothly. It's – well – most professional, if you see what I mean.'

He did see what she meant, and it pleased him. She had used the word he had applied in his mind to the photographs. The compliment gave him more pleasure coming from her than it would have done if it had been offered by a more qualified critic.

'Is there anything you'd like altered?'

'I don't think so.'

'There's nothing important I've left out?'

'No. You seem to have got it all in.'

'Well, like I said, it may have to be cut. But I'll let you see the final version before I submit it anywhere.'

That way, he thought, I get to see her again. And I'll go on seeing her to give progress reports. Things could not have been going better from his point of view. And all because of that spur of the moment suggestion he had made at their second encounter.

A Wind on the Heath

Soon he was seeing her almost on a regular basis. It cut into the time he could spend on his other writing, but he did not care. There appeared to be no other man in her life at the present time, and this was a fact that he found quite remarkable but which pleased him greatly. She seemed to enjoy being in his company, and he was never so happy as when he was with her.

She had told him that she was living in a flat but she had never invited him to visit it. One evening, however, he took her to see his place in Rosetta Avenue. She gave it a pretty thorough inspection but made no remark, and her expression was enigmatic. He waited for some verdict, but when none was forthcoming he said:

'Well? What do you think of it?'

She shrugged. 'It's all right, I suppose. For you.'

'What's wrong with it?'

'Nothing. Didn't I say it was all right?'

'Yes. For me. Why just for me?'

She smiled. 'Now I've upset you, haven't I?'

'No, you haven't. I'm not upset.'

'No? Well, what I meant was it's not exactly a luxury suite, is it?'

He admitted that it was not. 'But it's the best I can afford. I'm a struggling free-lance writer, remember.'

'Yes, of course. But one day you'll be rich and famous, won't you? Then you'll be able to live in style. Rolls-Royce, private yacht, holidays on the Riviera, that sort of thing. Promise you'll take me with you.'

'I promise,' he said. 'But by that time of course you'll be rich and famous too. You and me, a couple of millionaires.'

They both laughed, sharing the impossible dream; the dream that so many people had when they were young and hopeful and disillusionment had not yet come like a winter frost.

He introduced her to the Lakoses. She thought them odd but charming. They took to her at once. She had that way with people, making them like her on sight; or, as in his case, love her.

'It is so nice,' Petra said to him next day, 'for you to have a young lady. And she is so sweet, so attractive, so chic. As I say to Peter, she will be just right for him. They are a perfect pair. That is what I say, and he agrees. We are so happy for you.'

'Thank you,' Sterne said. 'That's very nice of you. But she's not really my young lady, you know. I am writing her story as a magazine feature. It's a business arrangement, nothing more.'

She gave a knowing smile. 'Oh, of course. Oh, indeed yes. And the way you look at her and the way she look at you, that is also a business arrangement? Come, come, David! Do not imagine you can pull the wool over my eyes. You must remember I am clairvoyant. But there is no need of clairvoyance to see when two young people are in love.'

'So you think she is in love with me?'

'I am sure of it. Are not you?'

He hoped she was right. He just hoped she was. But he was not so sure. Maybe. But then again, maybe not.

*

He had written the article. He had polished it until it could be polished no further and he had begun to send it out to possible markets. It came back. It came back time after time. After each successive rejection he felt more depressed, and the worst part was having to break the news to Angela that he had failed yet again. She did not say that she was losing faith in him, but she looked disappointed and he felt that she had good reason to be.

'I'm sorry,' he said. 'I shouldn't have led you on. It wasn't fair to you. I should have warned you it might turn out like this.'

She was more magnanimous than he might have expected. 'You didn't promise anything. I'm certainly not blaming you. You wrote a fine piece, and if all these editors are too stupid to spot a good thing when they see it, that's their loss. There's nothing we can do about it.'

'But it's such a disappointment for you. That's what hurts me.'

'Don't let it. Life goes on. If the piece never gets into print neither of us will be any worse off than we were before you suggested it. You'll have lost a bit of time and labour. I'll have lost nothing, and I'll have found you.'

He gave her a quick glance, suspecting that she might be making game of him. 'You really count that as something on the credit side?'

'Well, for God's sake,' she said, 'what do you think?'

'I think I'm in love with you,' he said. And kissed her.

'I was beginning to wonder whether you'd ever get round to that,' she said. 'What kept you so long?'

'I don't know. Fear, maybe.'

She stared at him. 'Fear! Of me?'

'Of a brush-off.'

'Oh, my poor David,' she said, laughing, 'what am I to do with you?'

'Anything you like,' he told her. 'Anything whatever except give me the boot.'

*

The typescript was beginning to look somewhat travel-worn, and he decided to hammer out a fresh copy on the old L.C. Smith, which itself was getting a bit rickety. Amazingly, this did the trick at once, though it might simply have been coincidence. The time might just have come for the work to find a home.

He had to admit when he told Angela about it that the home was not very grand. It was a weekly magazine called *Women's View* and it was not one of the leaders in its field.

'It's rather down-market, I'm afraid.'

'Never mind. At least it's something.'

That was about as much as could be said for it, he thought. It was not going to make her a star overnight. In fact, as matters turned out, it had quite the opposite effect.

Three days after publication of the feature Angela turned up at the flat and said: 'Can I have a word with you, David?'

He thought she looked somewhat depressed, and he was surprised to see her because this should have been one of her working days; but he would have been pleased to see her at any time.

'I'm not interrupting your writing, am I?'

He had in fact been working on a story, but it had not been going well and he was not sorry to have an excuse for breaking off; especially this excuse. He closed the door and invited her to sit down.

'Would you like a cup of coffee?'

'Oh, you don't need to bother.'

'It's no bother. I was about to have one myself.'

'Then I will have one,' she said. 'I need something.'

This sounded odd, even rather ominous; but he went into the kitchenette and set about making the coffee, leaving her seated in one of the much-worn armchairs and looking the picture of dejection.

He brought the coffee and said: 'I thought you were on duty today.'

'Well, I'm not,' she said. She drank some of the coffee and added: 'And I won't be on tomorrow or the next day or the day after that.'

'Oh God!' he said. 'You don't mean –'

'Yes, I do mean it. I've had the push. I've been slung out on my ear.'
'Oh no!'
'Oh yes!'
'But why? You were one of the best. Damn it, you were *the* best. Why would they want to get rid of you?'

She drank some more coffee, hesitated, and then came out with the whole story. It appeared from what she said that the management had taken umbrage at something in the *Women's View* feature about her. In the first place they said they should have been consulted before she went ahead with it. She should have asked for their approval; which was a lot of nonsense, of course. And they considered that parts of it were derogatory; they showed the Windmill in a bad light.

'And because of that they gave you the sack?'
'Yes.'

He found it hard to believe. He could think of nothing in what he had written that had been at all critical of the Windmill, and he had a feeling that there must be more to it than she had revealed. Perhaps there had already been friction between her and the management, and this had been a handy excuse for getting rid of her. Her next words seemed to give some confirmation of this suspicion.

'Well,' she said, 'I'm not sorry. There was bound to be a flare-up sooner or later. I could see it coming. And now it has.'

Once again she drank some coffee and looked pensive.

'It is a bit awkward, though.'
'In what way?'
'I'm skint.'
'Ah!'

He thought this must be an exaggeration, but when she had outlined the situation he could see that it was not far from the truth. It appeared that she had always spent her money as fast as it came in, and there was nothing put by for a rainy day. She was in arrears with the rent of her flat, and her pay-off from the Windmill had been only just enough to cover this debt. So she could not stay there any longer.

'I really am in a fix.'

He could see that this was indeed so if everything was as she had related it. And it had to be. She wouldn't be lying to him, would she? He dismissed this thought as unworthy.

She said hesitantly: 'I was wondering if – just for a day or two of course – to give me a chance to take a look round and get things sorted out –'

She paused, looking at him, waiting.

He would have had to be pretty dense not to see what she was driving at. And he didn't have to think twice about it, because nothing could have pleased him more.

'But of course,' he said. 'Of course you can stay here. You can have the bedroom and I can use this old sofa. It'll be no problem at all.'

Her depression seemed to vanish in an instant, as if he had waved a magic wand and banished it.

'Oh, David,' she said, 'that is sweet of you. But of course you must have the bedroom. The sofa will do for me.'

'No, no. I won't hear of it.'

'Well, we'll see. We'll work something out.'

*

He went with her to lend a hand when she collected her luggage. There were two suitcases and a smaller bag. Neither of the Lakoses was anywhere to be seen when they returned to the house, so there was no necessity to make any explanation to them for the present. Tomorrow would be soon enough for that.

'You really are being ever so sweet about this,' she said. 'I don't know what I'd have done without you.'

'Well, if it comes to that, it's no more than I owe you. If I hadn't suggested writing that damned feature you'd never have got the sack and none of this would have been necessary. It's all my fault. Don't you see?'

'No, you mustn't think that. You couldn't have foreseen what would happen. So there's no reason at all for you to feel bad about it. I'm not blaming you at all.' She gave a mischievous kind of smile and added: 'Anyway, I think I may rather like it here when I get used to it.'

This seemed to be an implication that she was planning to make her stay last rather longer than the day or two she had originally mentioned. He noticed this but did not remark on it.

*

He discovered that sleeping on the sofa was a pretty wretched business. It was a piece of furniture which had never been designed for that purpose: it was both too short and too narrow, and it was impossible to get the bedclothes to stay in place; they kept sliding off on to the floor. It was well past midnight before he came even near to dozing off, and then a creaking sound brought him fully awake again.

A gleam of light was coming from the bedroom, and he guessed that the sound had been made by the opening of the door. And then a shape drifted into his line of vision and he saw that it was the girl. She was wearing a suit of pale blue pyjamas and she moved noiselessly to the sofa and stood looking down at him.

'You are awake, aren't you?' she said.

'I haven't been asleep.'

'As I thought. Me neither, actually.'

'Bed not comfortable?'

'Oh the bed's fine. It's not that. I just keep thinking about you out here on this wretched sofa, and I feel so guilty.'

'There's no need to.'

'But I do. So don't you think it's just a little bit silly when the bed's perfectly big enough for the two of us?'

'Well,' he said, 'when you put it like that I suppose it is.'

'So hadn't we better do something about it?'

'Yes,' he said, 'perhaps we had.'

Not that he found it any easier to get to sleep in the bed – for quite a while at least. There seemed to be so much else to do; so much that was far more enjoyable; that was in fact the very peak of ecstasy.

'Aren't you glad,' she whispered, 'that I came to you?'

'That,' he said, 'is a question that hardly needs an answer. But I'll give one just the same. Yes, yes, yes, yes, yes.'

Chapter Ten – A DIFFERENT STORY

Peter and Petra Lakos had no objection whatever to Sterne's sharing his flat with Miss Street. They were entirely without prudery in that respect. They thought it was very nice for him.

'Such a charming couple,' Petra said. 'It warms the heart to see two young people so happy.'

She was sorry to hear that Angela had lost her job, but was confident that she would soon get another one. In a way Sterne hoped that she would not; at least not for a while; since he would have less of her company if she did. But he saw that the present situation had its drawbacks, the chief of which was financial. She was earning nothing, and for the present he was having to provide for the two of them. This was all very well for a few weeks or even months, but it could not go on indefinitely. He was having to dip more and more deeply into his meagre capital, even though he was selling more stories and had established himself as a regular contributor to the *Bury and North Suffolk Morning Post*. These 'London Letters' from 'Our Own Correspondent' earned him a guinea apiece, which was useful but not riches.

He did not mention his money worries to Angela. She must have realised that he was not making a lot of money, but she might not have guessed quite how slender his means were. She was paying frequent visits to her agent, and occasionally he would fix up an audition for her, but so far nothing had come of these.

'It's a tough profession,' she told him. 'Survival of the fittest.'

'You could say the same about writing.'

'Yes,' she said, 'I suppose so.' And then: 'Look, David, if I'm being too much of a burden you must say so. I can pack up and go, you know.'

He was appalled by the possibility that she might do as she had suggested. 'Don't even think of it. I love having you here; you must know that.'

'And I love being here. But one can't live on love alone, can one?'

'We'll get by,' he said. 'Something will turn up.'

Which, he remembered, was rather what Mr Micawber used to say. And where did it get him?

'Perhaps we should ask Petra to look into her crystal ball and tell us what the future holds for us.'

'She doesn't do that sort of thing. She just makes contact with the other world.'

'You don't believe all that rubbish, do you?'

'No. But don't ever tell her I said so.'

*

One morning she said: 'Today, David, I'd like to take you to see my father and mother.'

He stared at her. 'What are you talking about? Your mother is dead and your father is in Yorkshire.'

She gave a grin. 'Wrong on both counts, darling.'

'But you told me –'

'I fibbed. Sorry, David. The fact is I made it all up. From start to finish.'

He was astounded. 'I don't believe it. You're just kidding me. You have to be.'

'I'm not. This is the truth I'm telling now.'

He could see that she was serious. 'So there's no Yorkshire parson in your life?'

She shook her head. 'I've never been there.'

He was gradually taking in the purport of what she was telling him. If there was no Yorkshire parson and no dead mother, how much of the rest of the story she had fed to him was true? He put the question bluntly to her.

'Very little, I'm afraid.'

'You mean to say you thought it all up as you went along? That time when I was taking notes.'

'Not entirely. It was more or less the story I'd been telling people about myself. It sounded more romantic than the truth. So I had it all more or less by heart and just repeated it to you.'

And he had got it into print for her. Now it was all down in black and white. And it was nothing but a fable.

'So why have you decided to come clean with me now?'

'I should have thought that was obvious. You're special aren't you? I just couldn't bear to keep you in the dark any longer.'

A Wind on the Heath

He was pleased to hear this, but he was uneasy about the fact that the false story had been published in the *Women's View* magazine, and he told her so.

She was airily unconcerned about that. 'Nobody expects to get the truth in those things – unless they're very simple-minded. What's it matter? It's just another story.'

He was not sure he went along with that – not entirely. But there was nothing to be done about it now. It was out of the question to write to the editor of *Women's View*, telling her that there had been a mistake and that there was no truth in the feature they had printed about Angela Street.

'I think,' he said, 'that you'd better give me the true facts about yourself now, don't you?'

'Of course,' she said. 'That was what I was going to do, wasn't it?'

So then she told him; told him the truth. Yet it was the other story, the figment of her imagination, that was to become accepted by all and sundry and to stick with her throughout her career. Apparently no one would ever take the trouble to make the journey north and seek out the parson in Brontë country who was reputedly her father. But after all, Yorkshire was a large county and she had never given any precise information regarding the situation of the vicarage from which she had made her escape at the tender age of fourteen years. So why bother?

The fact was that her real name was not Angela Street but Maggie Maggs. Her father had a small greengrocery shop in the East End, and her mother had been a chorus girl until a weight problem had put an end to that line of work, and she had been only too glad to accept Alfie Maggs's offer of marriage. He had been a good-looking young man and a smart dresser, while the mother had been quite a beauty.

Maggie was an only child and had been sent to dancing classes almost as a matter of course, both parents hoping, and indeed expecting, that she would eventually go on the stage. At a very early age she was performing in charity shows and displaying a precocious talent for the business. Her progress as she grew older had not been as eventful as she had painted it in that first account she had given to Sterne, though it had not been without its struggles and setbacks.

The change of name had been made with the full approval of Alfie and Queenie Maggs, who agreed that Angela Street sounded far more distinguished. Soon she had moved out of the East End to a small flat of her own, which was more convenient for the theatre world and all that went with it. Later there had been another reason for getting away, a more compelling one; but she did not tell him that. He was to find out in time, and it was to come as a shock; but for the present he was to remain blissfully ignorant of it.

She had shed her cockney accent with the original name. She was a gifted mimic, and the change had been easy to make. From the way she spoke now it would have been difficult to guess where her roots were.

'So now what do I call you?' he asked when she had reached the end of her narration. 'Angela or Maggie?'

She gave a laugh. 'Just call me darling. That's what I like best.'

*

The greengrocer and his wife were delighted to see their daughter. He got the impression that her visits were not very frequent. It occurred to him also that when she had lost her job and her flat she might have gone to them for help. They would certainly have been happy enough to take her in. They would probably have given her money to tide her over the hard times as well. In fact they would have been the obvious people to go to. And yet she had not; instead she had come to him. Why?

The only answer he could think of to that question was that this was what she had wanted to do; that she had had in her mind from the outset the intention of moving in with him. This conclusion pleased him. She had misled him, of course, by giving the impression that she had nowhere else to go, no one else to help her, the vicar being far away in Yorkshire and unlikely to feel inclined to be charitably disposed towards her anyway, but he did not give two pins about that; he was just glad.

The greengrocer's shop was in a rather slummy district of London which had suffered from the depression and where a large proportion of the population was living on the dole; but it looked reasonably prosperous. The Maggses had a flat above the shop. The rooms were small but cosy. There was nothing luxurious about the furnishing, nor any indication of poverty either. Sterne would have guessed that Alfie Maggs was not short of a bob or two even if many of his customers were finding the going rough.

They had arrived in the evening, just as the shutters were going up, and high tea was about to be put on the table. It was taken for granted that they would stay and share the meal.

Angela had introduced him and added: 'David is a writer. He's going to be famous.'

'Is that a fact?' Alfie said. He looked at Sterne with a hint of amusement, a twinkle in his eye. 'Is that really a fact?'

'It's an exaggeration,' Sterne said. 'I've no hope of it ever coming true.'

'But you should 'ave. What's the use of going on without 'ope? Me, I'll never amount to nothing, but youngsters like you an' 'er, you've got it all in front of you. You can reach the top.'

Angela gave a laugh. 'All right, Dad. We'll do it, just for you and Mum.'

Eating cold ham and salad in the little living-room on the first floor, Sterne found himself being pumped by Mr Maggs, who seemed to be the sort of man who would not be easily imposed on. It was quite obvious that he was sizing up this person his daughter had brought along, and trying to determine whether he was a good or a bad thing. Somehow the greengrocer got him talking about the farm and his early life.

'Never knew much about the country meself; 'ardly ever bin there. Might give it a go one of these fine days. Sell up and buy a little cottage out in the wilds.'

'Not you, Dad,' Angela said. 'You're a Londoner and you always will be. You'd be lost in the country.'

'Well, it was just a thought.'

Sterne noticed that Angela made no mention of the fact that she had had to give up her flat and had moved in with him, though she did say she had left the Windmill and was looking for somewhere else. He wondered how much the Maggses guessed. They asked no questions on that subject.

Mrs Maggs said she was sorry the Windmill job had come to an end, but she made no attempt to probe into the details of the matter.

'Still, I'm sure you'll not be resting for long. Not with your talent.'

*

'So what did you think of them?' Angela asked when they were on their way back to the flat in Rosetta Avenue.

'I liked them.'

'You really mean that?'

'Of course I mean it.'

'Good. They liked you too, you know. Mum told me in confidence that she thought you were a very nice young man. What do you say to that?'

He grinned. 'I'd say she has excellent taste. Your father grilled me a bit. I think he was running the rule over me.'

'He would. He has this thing about protecting me from the rogue male, and he's afraid I'll –' She stopped abruptly, as though catching herself on the point of saying something she had not intended.

'Afraid you'll what?'

'Oh, nothing. Nothing important.'

He thought it might have been more than that, but he did not press her to elaborate. Nevertheless, he felt a little prick of doubt, of uneasiness. He knew so little about her even now. There were gaps which had never been filled. The story was still incomplete.

He wondered why she had taken him to see her parents. Perhaps she wished to show him just what her roots were, so that he could never accuse her of concealing her origin from him. Perhaps there was a kind of bravado in it, as if she were challenging him to be critical. She need have had no fear of that; he had told her the truth: he did like Alfie and Queenie. They were the genuine article, no doubt about that.

There might perhaps have been another motive for paying the visit; a financial one. He had not actually seen any money change hands, but next day Angela bought a few items of new clothing, and it was not difficult to guess where the necessary cash had come from.

*

And so life went on: days of writing, writing, writing, and nights of ecstatic love-making, exploring every curve and mound and hollow of her glorious body with passionate sensuous delight beyond all imagining. And she as ardent as he; sinuous in her movements as a snake, making of each nocturnal encounter a reaching upward to the very zenith of desire.

It could not last. Perhaps in their hearts they knew it must end; that the very intensity of it made certain there must be a limit to its endurance. The hottest fires burn out most quickly.

And yet it was not this that brought the close; no gradual cooling that would one day cause them to face each other and ask the question: 'Where did it all go? We had something truly exquisite and now it's gone. So how was it lost?'

No, it was not like this. It was brought to a close while still among the peaks and not the foothills; while still nothing had cooled, no fire quenched, the flame still as brilliant as ever.

One day a man walked in and smashed the dream.

Chapter Eleven – SORRY

When Sterne went to answer the knock on the door he had no inkling of what was about to happen. When he thought about it afterwards he could not help but feel that he should have had a premonition; that some sixth sense should have warned him not to open the door, because to do so would be to let in something evil. The vibrations should have been felt through the wood; they should have impinged on his brain, warning him.

But there had been nothing.

And even if there had been, even if he had refused to open the door, he could not have kept that evil out. Eventually it would have found a way in. It was fate.

He opened the door and the man was standing there. The man looked at him but said nothing.

'Yes?' Sterne said.

'My name is Judas Raven,' the man said.

It was an odd name, Sterne thought. Maybe even a name of ill omen. But it meant nothing to him.

The man was a handsome devil, no doubt about that. He had black crinkly hair and he was lean-faced, with a thin blade of a nose and dark eyes. His complexion too was dark; there could have been gipsy blood in him. He was not tall, being slightly shorter than Sterne, but he held himself well. He looked hard; he looked hard as old iron. He looked like someone a man would be wise not to tangle with. He could be a mean bastard.

'So?' Sterne said.

'I'd like to have a talk,' Raven said. His voice was soft, with a strangely lilting quality about it; a London accent without doubt, but with subtle overtones that might have been picked up elsewhere.

'With me?'

'Yes, with you.'

'About what?'

'Maybe I'd better come in,' the man said. He was wearing a charcoal-grey suit that looked almost new and very smart. His black shoes were polished to a gleam. 'Best inside.'

Sterne did not wish to let him in, but there would have been something ridiculous in refusing to do so.

'Very well.'

Raven gave a quick glance round the living-room when he walked in. It was as though he were searching for something; but if so, it was evidently not there.

'You can sit down,' Sterne said, a trifle grudgingly.

Raven sat down. 'They tell me you're a writer, Mr Sterne.'

So the man knew his name; knew his occupation too. He wondered who 'they' were.

'That's so.'

'I'm looking for someone,' Raven said.

It gave Sterne a jolt. The thought that sprang immediately into his mind was that this someone Raven was speaking about was Angela. Who else could it be? And he knew exactly where she was at that moment: she was taking a bath. And the bathroom was just two doors away: you went through the bedroom to get to it.

'The name of the person,' Raven said, 'is Angela Street.'

Which was immediate confirmation of what Sterne had suspected. He wondered whether the man had noticed his involuntary reaction when he had stated that he was looking for someone. Probably. There was that about him which suggested that he would not miss much and would not easily be fooled.

But why would he be looking for her? Who in hell was he? She had never mentioned that name. But probably there were a lot of things she had never mentioned. Perhaps Alfie Maggs could have told him quite a bit about Judas Raven if he had asked.

He spoke warily, hoping Miss Street would take some time over her bath; hoping he could get rid of this man before she walked out of the bedroom.

'Why have you come to me?'

'I'll tell you,' Raven said. 'I've been away. You don't have to know where; it ain't important. I come back and I've lost touch, if you see what I mean. I try to pick up the threads, but it looks like things have changed. I pay a call on her flat as used to be, and it's in different hands now and the people ain't never heard of her. So then I go to the Windmill Theatre where she used to perform, and they tell me she ain't working there no more and they don't know where she's living. It looks like a dead end, and

I'm just leaving when they say why not try this magazine called *Women's View*, 'cause there was a piece about her in it not long ago and they might know where she is.'

Raven paused and stared hard at Sterne.

Sterne said: 'And did they?'

'No, they didn't. But they remember the piece and they hunt up the name and address of the man who wrote it. And of course it's as clear as daylight he must've been in contact with her and would maybe know where she's hanging out right now.'

Once again Raven paused and gave Sterne a hard cold stare, as if boring into him with his eyes.

Then he said: 'You did write that piece, didn't you?'

'Yes, I did.'

'And you know where Miss Street is now?'

Sterne knew only too well, but he did not wish to tell Raven. He wondered why the man had not got in touch with Alfie Maggs. But perhaps he had and had got no change out of him. Or perhaps he had known he would get just that and had not even tried. He didn't know whether Angela would have wanted to see him, but he knew that he himself would be happier if the meeting did not take place. He could see no good coming from it and possibly a great deal of bad. He did not like the look of Raven. His guess was that he was not a man to be trusted.

So he said: 'No, I don't.'

'You can't help me?'

'No.'

Raven did not believe him; that much was obvious. He said: 'But you must have had contact with her when you were writing about her.'

'Of course. But that was when she was living at the flat. Now you say she isn't there any more.'

'Are you saying you don't know her new address?'

'That's it. No idea. And now I've got work to do, so if you don't mind –'

He thought for a moment that Raven would refuse to leave. But then he got up from the chair and walked to the door. He turned with his hand on the knob.

'I'll find her,' he said, and he sounded vehement. 'I'll find her if it's the last thing I do. She's my girl; do you know that?'

'No,' Sterne said. And he did not want to know it; did not want to believe it. 'No.'

'Well, she is. And anybody that says different had better watch his step. He bloody well had better, I'm telling you.'

He twisted the knob viciously, as though he might have been wringing the neck of some person unknown, and pulled the door open.

And that was the moment when Angela chose to come in from the bedroom. She was wearing a dressing-gown and mules, and her hair looked damp.

Raven heard the sound, turned and saw her. He slammed the door shut again and she gave a cry.

'You!'

'Yes, me,' he said. 'Surprise, surprise!' He rounded on Sterne with a kind of snarl. 'You lied to me. You bloody lied to me. What in hell's going on?'

He received no answer.

'Well,' he sneered, 'it's easy to see, ain't it? She's been living here. Left her flat and moved in with you. That's nice.'

Angela said: 'You don't understand, Jude.'

'Oh,' he said, 'I understand all right. Couldn't wait for me, could you?'

'Jude, it's been a long time.' She seemed to be pleading with him, and Sterne could tell that she was nervous, perhaps fearful of this man who had stepped back into her life so unexpectedly. 'Things change.'

'Oh yes,' Raven said, 'it's been a long time sure enough. You don't need to tell me how long. And I'll bet it's been one hell of a lot longer for me than it has for you. But it's over now. I'm back and I've come for you. Get dressed and pack your bags and we'll be on our way.'

'Now hold on,' Sterne said. 'She's not going anywhere. You've got a nerve barging in here and dishing out your orders. Get out of here. Go on. Get out.'

Raven moved so fast then that he had no time to guess what was about to happen. Something seemed to explode in his right eye with a brilliant display of stars, and it was not until later that he realised it was the man's iron fist. He went down, upsetting a chair on the way. He was blind in one eye and the pain was agonising. As if from a long distance he heard the girl scream. He was dazed and only half aware of a knee on his chest and a knife pricking his throat. He was seeing none too clearly from his one good eye, but he had a vague impression of Raven's face hovering over him and words spilling out of the mouth in vicious little spurts.

A Wind on the Heath

'I could kill you, you bastard. People get in my way, they wish they hadn't. Maybe I carve you up some; spoil your looks; learn you not to get in my way. How'd you like that, mate?'

'No, Jude, no!' It was Angela's voice. She was pleading with him; fearing what he might do in his rage. 'Please! Oh, please!'

He took no notice of her.

'This for a start,' he said.

Sterne felt the blade of the knife make a cut in the flesh under his chin. It was to leave a scar that would be with him for the rest of his life. He tried to struggle free but was groggy from the blow that had almost stunned him, and Raven's knee was heavy on his chest. He waited for the next cut to be made.

But it never came.

Another voice broke in: 'Drop the knife or I will shoot you through the head.'

It sounded like Lakos's voice, though it was crisper and more authoritative than he had heard it sound before. And then, through the kind of gauzy screen which was blurring his vision, he discerned Lakos standing close to Raven and pointing a stubby revolver at his head.

He could not believe it. Peter Lakos was the last person he would have suspected of owning a weapon of that kind and of being prepared to use it. Could it be that he was in dreamland and imagining all this?

But then Lakos said: 'Do it. I shall not tell you again.'

Raven must have decided that the threat was genuine, or at least that it would be advisable not to take a chance on its being merely bluff. He put the knife down on the floor and stood up, removing the pressure of his knee from Sterne's chest.

'You wouldn't use that thing,' he said. 'An old bastard like you.' But he did not sound too sure.

'I may be an old bastard,' Lakos said. 'but you will find out whether I would use this gun if you do not leave my house this instant. I have killed men for less than you have done. So now away with you.'

Raven seemed to be in half a mind to refuse. He might have been thinking of calling Lakos's bluff – if it was a bluff. But in the end he lacked the nerve. The gun was too close and there was a finger on the trigger.

'All right,' he said, 'I'll go.' But before leaving he spoke again to the girl. 'I want you back, Mag. I mean to have you back. You better not be obstinate; it could be the worse for him.' He stabbed a finger at Sterne. 'You get me?'

She said nothing.

He felt in his pocket and fished out a card. It was not printed but an address had been written on it in block capitals. He flicked it towards her and it fell at her feet.

'That's where you'll find me. Don't keep me waiting too long. You know me. No patience.'

'Go,' Lakos said. 'You are trying my patience.'

Raven made an obscene gesture and went.

*

Sterne's eye plagued him all night in spite of cold compresses applied by Angela and some kind of concoction prepared by Petra Lakos. In the morning it looked bad and he knew it was going to be bad for days, maybe even weeks. The cut under his chin had bled a lot, but it was not too serious and it was covered now with a strip of sticking-plaster.

He asked Lakos what had made him come up to the flat with the revolver. Lakos said that it was a feeling he had had.

'It was I who let that man into the house, and I saw at once that he was a rogue; I have an eye for such things. I saw him enter your flat and feared there might be trouble. So I climbed the stairs and listened at the door. In the end I heard enough to make me think it was time I intervened; so I went in.'

'And you had the gun with you?'

'Oh yes. I knew that if there was trouble I would be of no use without a weapon. I am not a man of violence. I cannot use my fists like a pugilist.'

'I am surprised you own a gun,' Sterne said. He wondered whether the revolver was registered, but he did not ask.

'There are reasons,' Lakos said. But it was apparent that he had no intention of saying what those reasons were.

'And is it true that you have killed men?'

Lakos smiled. 'Oh no, no. Do I look like a killer? That was just to persuade the man that he had better not hang around. I don't know whether he believed it, but it made him think.'

'Are you going to tell the police about this?' Sterne asked.

Lakos answered quickly: 'No. I don't think that will be necessary, do you?'

'No, perhaps not,' Sterne said. He was thinking of Angela becoming involved. Better not to have the coppers putting their noses into the affair.

*

Later Angela said: 'You want to know all about him, don't you?'

He had asked no questions, but she was right: he did want to know. He had heard enough to make him unhappy, and he guessed that whatever else she might tell him would be likely to make him even more so. But he had to know.

'You know where he's been, don't you?'

'No, I don't. Abroad?'

She gave a hard sort of laugh. 'No, not abroad. In stir.'

'Stir?'

'Prison.'

'Oh!'

'I didn't know he was out until he turned up here.'

'What was he in for?'

'Robbery with violence.'

'I see.' So violence was part of his stock-in-trade. Well, that came as no surprise. He had given a demonstration of it. 'Was it right what he said – that you were his girl?'

She admitted that it was. 'We practically grew up together, though he's a few years older than me. I thought he was wonderful; he was my hero; he used to be top dog with all the other boys. Then when I started dancing professionally I left home and went to live with him. He was making pots of money one way and another, and he had a lovely flat.'

'Better than this, I imagine.'

'Yes, but –'

He could imagine a lot more; imagine that swine and her together, making love. It hurt. It hurt him more than his injured eye, which was surrounded by black and swollen bruises; a real shiner.

'What did your people think of you going to live with him?'

'They didn't like it at all. They never had liked him.'

Well, good for them, he thought. It showed better judgement on their part than she had shown.

*

She was restless all day. He knew that she was thinking about Judas Raven, and it bothered him. He caught her looking at the card Raven had thrown at her.

He said: 'Don't even think of it. Don't even think of it for a moment.'

'I have to,' she said.

'You can't mean it. You can't really mean you're considering the possibility of leaving me and going back to that swine. I don't believe it.'

It was a shock to hear that it had even entered her head. But obviously it had, and he had to face the fact, distasteful though it might be.

'It would maybe be for the best, you know.'

'How can you say that?'

'Well, look at it this way. If I don't do what he wants he'll take it out on you. From his point of view you're an interloper. He's jealous as hell and he'll stop at nothing to get rid of you. You've got to realise that.'

'So what can he do? Kill me?'

'Even that wouldn't be out of the question. But probably the start would be a beating-up. He wouldn't even have to do the job himself; he knows the sort of people who'd do that sort of thing any day of the week if they were paid to. And they'd give you a real going-over. It'd be more than just a black eye and a broken tooth. You'd be a hospital case. Believe me, David, I know about these things and I don't think you do.'

'I can take care of myself.'

'You may think so, but you can't. However careful you were, they'd get you in the end.'

He thought about it. He thought about it for a whole minute, and his thoughts were gloomy.

'So what you're saying is that if you were to go back to him you'd be doing it entirely for my sake? To save me from getting hurt. Is that it?'

'Yes, that is it.'

He gave her a keen searching look, and it came to him like a sudden blinding revelation; the truth of the matter.

'I don't believe you. You're not thinking of me; you're thinking of yourself. You're still in love with him, aren't you? You want to go back to him.'

She said nothing; made no vehement denial of the charge; just met his accusing gaze in silence.

'So it's true. It's true, isn't it?'

'If you say so,' she said.

He lost his temper. He had an impulse to hit her. She was so cool, and her coolness maddened him, nearly drove him out of his mind. But with a supreme effort of self-control he restrained the impulse and even managed to speak calmly, though bitterly.

'Very well, then. You'd better go.'

'I'm sorry, David.'

Sorry! She was sorry! It didn't even begin to describe how he felt.

Chapter Twelve – ARREST

In the late summer of 1939 he decided to join the Territorial Army. Anyone who was not blind and deaf or half-witted could tell that war was inevitable, and he felt that he had to do something about it. Hitler was insatiable. In March he had annexed Bohemia and Moravia, making them a German Protectorate. In April his ally, Mussolini, had seized Albania. Austria had already gone, Poland was threatened, and there seemed to be no end to the land-grabbing by the two fascist powers. Somebody surely had to make a stand, if it was only David Sterne.

It was now five months since Angela had left, and he had neither seen nor had a word from her in all that time. He supposed she was still with Raven. He could no doubt have obtained information regarding her from the Maggses if he had taken a trip down to the East End where the greengrocer's shop was situated, but he was not at all sure he wanted to have news of her. It could only serve to open the old wound, which had never fully healed. He still missed her. He could never get her out of his mind; remembering the sweetness of life with her and regretting that it had had to come to an end.

There was just one favourable result of it: he now had no distraction from his writing. Successes still came with little frequency, but he was learning his trade; he was learning all the time. And now once again he could live with a frugality that had rather gone by the board while there had been two of them in the flat.

The Lakoses had been saddened by the departure of his partner. They both had an affection for Angela, and they could not imagine how she could have brought herself to abandon him in favour of that other man.

'A scoundrel,' Peter said. 'A villain. One could see it at a glance. And she has gone to him. What madness. What could she see in him?'

'They had been lovers since childhood,' Sterne said. 'I suppose her time with me was just an interlude while he was away.'

Mrs Lakos refused to believe it. 'She was in love with you. How can you doubt it? I tell you what it is: there is witchcraft in this. He has bewitched her; made her crazy.'

'I should have shot him,' Lakos said. 'I should have shot him when I had the chance. A man like that has no right to live.'

Sterne had to laugh. The idea of Peter Lakos shooting anyone was too ludicrous; not to be taken seriously.

'Perhaps someone else will kill him,' Petra said. 'There is always hope. I am sure he has many enemies.'

*

The unit that Sterne joined was a light anti-aircraft battery. He now had the rank of gunner and a number: 1489116. He had a battledress uniform made of coarse khaki material and a pair of ammunition boots with hobnails in the soles and irons on the heels. When you marched in such boots on a hard surface they made a clinking noise which beat out the rhythm of the march and helped you to keep in step with the other men in the column. He liked route marches; there was a camaraderie about them that was unique and wholly pleasurable.

In that glorious late summer before the world went mad he did foot-drill and rifle-drill and gun-drill on the Bofors. He learned about aim-off and cartwheel sights and moving targets and the intricate mechanism of the 40 millimetre quick-firing gun with its long slim barrel and conical flash-guard on the end.

When he told the Lakoses that he had joined the Territorials he was not sure whether they approved or not. They both looked rather concerned.

'You think there will be a war?' Peter asked.

'It looks pretty certain, doesn't it? What do you think?'

'I am afraid you may be right. It will be a disaster of course.'

'But somebody has got to stop the Nazis.'

'Yes, that is true.'

Mrs Lakos said: 'I cannot bear to think of you going to fight, David.'

'But if there's to be any fighting I couldn't just leave it to others.'

'But you need not have put yourself forward.'

'Perhaps not. But it would probably have come to it in the end.'

He had of course told his parents. His mother tended to think along the same lines as Mrs Lakos; it worried her. His father thought he had done the right thing and was proud of him. Whatever opinions George and Will might have had on the subject were not revealed to him. He doubted whether they were either proud or worried.

*

It was an odd thing that on the very day, August the 23rd, when Ribbentrop and Molotov signed the infamous German-Soviet treaty which effectually carved up Poland between the two great dictatorships and gave each of them time to prepare to fight the other, Peter and Petra Lakos were arrested. It was sheer coincidence of course; the two events were not connected in any way and took place fifteen hundred miles apart, but Sterne always remembered the two in tandem because they had occurred on the same day.

It was also the day when he glanced out of the window and saw the couple meditating on the grass patch below. Later he saw them picking up their things and returning to the house.

About half an hour more had passed when the police turned up. He heard the cars stopping in the street outside, and in a minute the house seemed to be full of policemen, some in plain clothes, others in uniform. Some of them came rushing up the stairs, and the door of the flat was pushed open without the preliminary of a knock and two of the officers came in.

'What's going on?' Sterne demanded.

One of the men, who was wearing a grey suit and trilby hat, said: 'I'm Detective Sergeant Blake.' He showed a warrant card. 'And this is Constable Foan.'

Foan was in uniform. He was standing with his back to the door, as if to make sure that Sterne did not make a run for it.

'What is your name, sir?' Blake asked.

Sterne told him.

'And you live here?'

'Yes. I rent this flat from Mr Lakos.'

'Is there anyone else living here?'

'No. I'm on my own. But what is this?'

Blake ignored the question and said: 'We'll just check up if you don't mind, sir.'

He gave a nod to the constable, who then made a rapid inspection of the bedroom and the kitchenette and found no one hiding anywhere. Sterne could hear the sound of heavy feet in the attic above, so it was obvious that a search was going on up there also.

'I wish you'd explain,' he said. 'What am I supposed to have done?'

Again Blake failed to answer the question. Instead, he asked one of his own: 'What do you do for a living, sir?'

'I'm a writer.'

'Oh, a writer, are you?' Blake said. Somehow or other he succeeded in making this sound highly suspicious.

'Yes,' Sterne said. 'If you don't believe me, ask Mr Lakos. He'll tell you the same.'

'Oh, no doubt. I am sure Mr Lakos will tell us a very great deal. And Mrs Lakos also. But it will be at the station. They are both under arrest.'

'Under arrest! But what have they done?'

'You don't know?'

'Of course I don't know. I can't think of anything they would be arrested for. They are two perfectly respectable people.'

'Oh yes, very respectable.' Blake spoke ironically. 'We are always arresting respectable people. They usually turn out to be the worst kind.'

A little later Sterne found himself in a police car being taken to the station from which the officers had come. There he was questioned about his relations with the Lakoses, and eventually he discovered why they had been arrested. It appeared that they were part of a spying operation, though they did none of the collecting of information themselves. Secret agents came to the secondhand bookshop and passed material to Lakos, who transmitted it in coded messages to Berlin. The radio equipment in the attic of Number 23, Rosetta Avenue was a short-wave transmitter, and what Lakos had passed off as a harmless hobby had a darker side to it. Mrs Lakos was also deeply involved in the operation.

Sterne found all this hard to believe; it seemed so out of character. How could those two pleasant innocent-seeming people be part of a Nazi espionage organisation? Had not Peter been thrown into a paroxysm of fury at the mere sound of the Fuehrer's voice coming out of the Cossor? Had he not called the man a monster and a maniac?

But when he mentioned this to Blake the detective sergeant gave a shake of the head and a cynical smile. 'You shouldn't let yourself be fooled, Mr Sterne. When you are dealing with a man as cunning as Lakos you have to look beneath the surface. You have to strip away the innocent front presented to you and uncover the true picture concealed behind.'

Sterne was forced to accept the truth of what Blake was saying. The proof was in the radio transmitter hidden in the attic of that unpretentious house on Rosetta Avenue, in the code books found with it, in the evidence of an agent intercepted coming from the bookshop who had decided that it was in his own best interests to turn informer and put the finger on Peter Lakos.

And then he remembered the man he himself had seen in Lakos's shop; the man in a black raincoat and a black felt hat. He remembered the man's eyes that had held his own for a moment, and how he had felt unnerved. He remembered too that Lakos had seemed uneasy and had told him that he would have to leave. There had also been the matter of the revolver with which he had threatened Judas Raven. Would an ordinary law-abiding citizen have owned such a weapon? And would a law-abiding citizen have been so opposed to the idea of reporting the incident to the police? His reluctance to take any action of that kind was perfectly explicable now. He would not have wished to attract the attention of those gentlemen.

But would anyone engaged in such a criminal activity as passing secret information to a foreign power have taken the risk of letting to another person the flat immediately below the attic where the transmitter was installed? Surely not.

He put this also to Sergeant Blake and was told that it was quite likely. 'It would reinforce the innocent appearance of the establishment. The séances and meditation and all that sort of thing could have been for the same purpose. A smokescreen. Oh, they're a sly pair, those two.'

Sterne had by this time succeeded in convincing the sergeant and his superiors that he himself was innocent. They had no evidence pointing to his involvement in the espionage, and the fact that he had recently joined the Territorial Army counted in his favour.

'Though,' Blake said with a grin, 'that could have been a blind too, couldn't it?'

He was not allowed to see the Lakoses before leaving. He asked Blake what would happen to them, and the detective gave a shrug.

'They'll be put behind bars for a good long time. You can count on that.'

Sterne felt saddened. It seemed a terrible prospect. How would they stand up to it? He still felt there must be some explanation for what they had done. But what possible explanation could there be except the obvious one that they were dyed-in-the-wool Nazis? And he would never understand how two such likable people could be that.

It was to be several years before he learned the whole truth of the matter. And by then one of the couple was dead and the other was close to dying.

Chapter Thirteen – MIRACLE

A few days later he had other things to occupy his mind. Britain was at war with Germany and he was a full-time soldier. More than six years were to pass before he could return to civilian life. People were saying that it would be all over by Christmas; but which Christmas? That was the question.

He spent the first Christmas of the War in Northern France, not far from the Maginot Line and the Belgian border. Life was uncomfortable but not particularly dangerous. The most notable thing that had happened to him was the award of his first stripe, and he was now a lance-bombardier. It was a rank that carried with it a few more responsibilities and no noticeable advantages apart from a very small rise in pay from the fourteen shillings a week earned by a gunner.

It was the time of the so-called Phoney War. In fact it suited both sides to have little activity on the Franco-German frontier: the British used the lull to continue rearming and the Germans were happy with a quiet Western Front while they dealt with Poland and prepared for a spring offensive against the Allies.

Not that all was quiet. At sea there never had been anything phoney about the conflict. Surface raiders and U-boats were sinking British ships in large numbers; the battleship *Royal Oak* had been sunk in Scapa Flow; and the Battle of the River Plate had ended in the scuttling of the German battleship *Admiral Graf Spee*. Meanwhile, Russia had invaded Finland, and after initial reverses had overpowered the small Finnish army by sheer weight of numbers. As a result the Finns lost the Karelia Isthmus and more besides.

But where Sterne was nothing much was happening, and this state of affairs continued into the New Year. Even when the Germans invaded Norway on April the Tenth and Britain sent an ill-fated expeditionary force to help the Norwegians and suffered ignominious defeat, this had little effect on him. Life went on in much the same way: monotonous, unexciting, boring.

All this abruptly changed early in May when the German blitzkrieg was suddenly launched with the invasion of Holland, Belgium and Luxemburg. The Maginot Line, which was supposed to have protected France, became an irrelevance overnight, since the German army had simply bypassed it at the northern end by way of the neighbouring country.

In the ensuing three weeks life for him became hectic and confusing. He had become one small part of an army in full retreat. The BEF was withdrawing, and he as an individual soldier knew nothing of the grand design or even if there was one. To him it seemed more and more like panic flight rather than an orderly withdrawal.

There was a sergeant named Holmes in command of the gun team, and it was not long before they became separated from the rest of the troop. They rode in the truck that hauled the gun for the first part of the journey, and everywhere the houses had white sheets hanging from the windows, the inhabitants knowing that the Germans were coming and already preparing to make their peace with them. Collaboration was on the way.

Others were fleeing, not willing to trust the invader. The roads were crammed with refugees using all kinds of transport: cars, lorries, horse-drawn carts and trollies, handcarts, prams, bicycles, anything on wheels. All that they could carry they were taking with them: bedding, furniture, bundles of clothing, pots and pans. Old men, women, children, all were on the move towards some unknown destination, leaving behind their homes and heading for they knew not what. Instinct told them to flee from the terror advancing from the east and the north, and they fled blindly in fear and desperation.

And through this ruck of terror-stricken humanity the retreating armies, French, British and Belgian, struggled to force their way. Trucks, Bren-gun carriers, half-tracks, staff cars, artillery were all streaming in one direction, away from the enemy.

The dive-bombers, the Stukas with their cranked wings and their banshee wailing came to add to the confusion and terror, and there was scarcely time to set up the Bofors gun and fire back before the planes had dropped their bombs and gone. The carnage was fearful; civilians and soldiers were slaughtered together; children and grand-parents cut to pieces in the same explosion. But when the planes had gone the column moved on, the wreckage shifted aside, the dead abandoned.

On the fifth day Sergeant Holmes was killed by a bullet from a strafing Messerschmidt and Sterne had to take command of the little detachment of gunners. Gradually the countryside altered in appearance and they came to a region of low-lying fields with a network of canals and roadways dividing the land into squares and rectangles. The ground was marshy and the road they were following ran straight through it, with dykes on either side and a few pollarded trees. Into this flat soggy area the retreating armies seemed to be converging, and the entire landscape was marked by the drab-coloured columns that moved so slowly towards their destination which, according to the word that had gone round, was to be the port of Dunkirk.

One day when they were still some way from the journey's end the order came through that the gun and the truck were to be broken up so that they should not fall into the hands of the enemy. Everywhere equipment was being destroyed with sledge-hammers and crowbars, tyres slashed with knives or saws, radio apparatus wrecked, motor engines smashed to pieces. The Bofors gun and the truck that had hauled it did not escape this mayhem; that which they had cherished for so long, maintaining it in perfect condition with so much devotion, was now to be completely ruined beneath the frenzied blows of a hammer. It was vandalism by order.

'It's a bleedin' shame,' Gunner Smith said. He was a little runt of a man, generally known as Smith 124, these being the last three digits in his army number, to distinguish him from Smith 493 who was also in the troop. 'People went to a lotta trouble making that there gun and now it comes to this. It won't never get put together again.'

'That,' Sterne said, 'is the object of the exercise.'

'I know. But it ain't right. It's like we was turning on an old friend an' givin' 'im a kick in the teeth.'

Sterne would not have expected him to have so much sentiment; he had never shown any affection for the gun when there had been work to do on it. But you never knew how people would react in any unforeseen situation.

*

They had to walk those last miles to Dunkirk, though in fact it was not to the port itself that they were to go, but to the seaside resort of Malo-les-Bains which adjoined it. The last part of the way found them stumbling through sand-dunes as the light faded. They were not the first to reach the beaches; the evacuation operation had already been in progress for three days, and the first thing that struck Sterne as they came through the dunes was the stench of rotting flesh. The beaches had been shelled continually and attacked from the air, and there were dead bodies everywhere. There were wounded and dying men lying around on the sand, many horribly mutilated by shell splinters. From here and there out of the gloom came a low moaning sound, punctuated by sudden quivering screams of pain.

Down towards the edge of the sea three fairly widely separated lines could just be discerned extending a short distance from the shore. These were the queues of men standing in pairs and waiting patiently for the small boats that would ferry them to the larger craft anchored offshore in deeper water. The queues were very orderly, like people waiting outside a cinema or theatre, and they gave the impression of being groynes or jetties, apparently just as motionless.

A curious fact was that this was not the first occasion when Sterne had been on this beach; but the previous time had been in far different circumstances. He had been about fifteen years old then, and had come to Dunkirk with a party of schoolboys in the summer holiday. They had stayed for two weeks in an old boarding-school named after the seventeenth century French Admiral Jean Bart who was born in the town, and they had walked daily to another school for instruction in the language of the country. Not that his mastery of French, never very great, had improved much as a result, but there had been outings and games and plenty of free time, which made the operation worth while from his point of view.

He remembered an outing by bus when they had crossed the frontier into Belgium and had visited Ypres. They had seen some of the old trenches of that other war, with the dugouts and the barbed wire, preserved perhaps as a warning to later generations – a warning unfortunately that had gone unheeded. They had visited the Menin Gate with its columns of names of men who had died in those bloody battles years ago, when there had been another retreat – from Mons. An angel had appeared to those men, so it was said, protecting them. He had seen no angel this time.

They had gone swimming from this very beach, he and some of the other boys. There had been bathing-machines on the sands then. You got inside where you could change your clothes in decent seclusion, and a horse was harnessed to the machine and it was dragged down on its wheels to the water. When you had finished bathing you got back into the machine and raised a small flag on the top by means of a cord. Then the attendant brought the horse and you were conveyed back up the beach. He could see no bathing-machines now, but perhaps they were there somewhere. He could just discern the long promenade where they had walked and cast glances at the pretty girls in their white dresses and summer hats.

It was all so different now: no pretty girls, no white dresses, just the remnants of a defeated army waiting to be rescued.

He and his men were on the beach for two days. They were two days of sheer hell; of shelling, bombing and strafing, getting what little shelter they could by digging shallow holes in the sand.

In the end they were taken off by one of the armada of little ships that came across the Channel to join in the work of rescue. The boat which took them was a private motor-cruiser commanded by an elderly grey-haired man wearing a yachting cap, blue blazer and white trousers. His crew was a boy of sixteen who turned out to be his grandson. Both were remarkably cool in the circumstances and seemed to know exactly what to do. Twenty-five survivors were packed in somehow and transported to Ramsgate.

Smith 124 put his own feelings pretty accurately into words. 'Strewth,' he said, 'I thought we was bloody goners, for sure. It's a miracle, that's what it is. A bloody miracle.'

'For once, Smithie,' Sterne said, 'I think you're right.'

It was not until years later that he was to learn how much Adolf Hitler himself had contributed to this miracle. Receiving reports of the progress of the campaign at the headquarters of the Supreme Command far away in Berlin, the Fuehrer had decided to ignore the recommendations of Field-Marshall von Runstedt, the man in command on the spot, and forbid the sending in of the panzer divisions for a final assault on Dunkirk. His reason apparently was that he feared his tanks might get bogged down in the marshy ground and suffer heavy losses. So the German army halted ten kilometres from the town and waited while 224,585 British and 112,546 French and Belgian troops, who might have been killed or captured, were spirited away under their very noses. The effect of this incredible blunder on the subsequent course of the war was incalculable.

What was quite certain, however, was that it enabled a certain Lance-Bombardier David Sterne to live to fight another day.

Chapter Fourteen – EMBARKATION

Soon after his return to England and a spell of leave Sterne was posted to a light anti-aircraft battery which was stationed in East Anglia. There were four gun-sites at points along the perimeter of an airfield from which Blenheim light bombers were operating. The Bofors guns were there to defend the airfield from low-level attacks by German bombers, but in all the time he was stationed there not one bomb fell anywhere near.

He had been promoted to the rank of full bombardier and his pay had gone up, but it had to be admitted that the life was unexciting, and indeed deadly boring. He lived in a wooden hut with half a dozen other men, and they went through the same routine day after day. They cleaned the gun, they did gun-drill, they watched the skies for the marauders that never came, they saw the Blenheims taking off on missions and saw them return – those that did return. They polished buttons and cap badges and blancoed webbing. They had visits from the lieutenant, the captain, the major and occasionally the colonel. They kept in the hut a Lewis gun and several pans of .303 ammunition for use in defending the site in the event of enemy paratroops descending on the airfield. None of them had ever fired a Lewis gun and no paratroops came.

He went on courses. He learned all about gas warfare and came to the conclusion that if poison gas were ever used life would become intolerable. He doubted whether the gas-cape which was standard issue would really be much good at protecting him from mustard gas or lewisite.

It was a white Christmas. It was the second one of the War and people had stopped saying it would all be over by Christmas; everybody knew it would be a long haul and they were resigned to it. No one that he knew seemed to think for a moment that Britain would lose the War; but looking at the hard facts it was difficult to see how it could ever be won. It was a case of blind faith overcoming cold logic. Defeat was unthinkable.

*

In the spring of 1941 Sterne decided to volunteer for a unit that was being formed to man Bofors guns on board merchant ships. Hitherto their only defence against attacks from the air had been Lewis guns on high-angle mountings and Hotchkisses and Marlins and old twelve-pounders, together with a variety of Heath-Robinsonish devices such as rockets that carried up cables with small parachutes attached, designed to catch the wings of low-flying aircraft. It appeared that the output of Bofors guns from the ordnance factories was now sufficient to warrant the mounting of them on ships, and the various light anti-aircraft batteries around the country were being invited to supply the personnel to man them.

Thus it was that in May 1941 Bombardier David Sterne arrived with his kit at North Shields to join a battery that was later to become part of the Maritime Royal Artillery working in partnership with the Naval DEMS organisation, the initials standing for Defensively Equipped Merchant Ships. The battery was at the time accommodated in a number of requisitioned terrace houses facing a piece of waste ground. The battery office was at one end of the row, and it was here that he was interviewed by the captain who was in command and was soon to be promoted to the rank of major. This officer welcomed him to what appeared from his words to be one of the finest units in the British army.

'You are,' he said, 'joining a first class body of men. You, bombardier, will be given a gun-team and will go out from here to defend our shipping from the enemy. There can be no more important task than that. The convoys are this country's lifelines and if we lose the Battle of the Atlantic we're sunk.'

The captain had a staccato way of speaking and he obviously believed in the efficacy of the pep talk. He was also at pains to impress upon this latest addition to his force the splendid qualities of the battery he was joining.

A rather different version was given by a gunner who conducted him to the room where he was to sleep. It had been a bedroom in former days but probably never with so many occupants. The only furniture it contained was a number of two-tier timber-and-wire bunks. One of the upper bunks was vacant and Sterne took it.

'You've come to a right bloody shambles here, bom,' the gunner said. He was a sour-looking character who spoke with a kind of whine. 'Talk about Fred Karno's army! They ain't in it. Not with this lot.'

'That's odd,' Sterne said. 'The captain told me it was all first class.'

The gunner winked knowingly. 'He would, wouldn't he? Meanter say, it's his party, ain't it? Stands to reason he won't run it down. But you'll see.'

*

Next morning, on parade in the road outside the terrace, Sterne felt that the gunner might have been nearer to the truth than the captain. The men who had been ordered by a sergeant to fall in looked a motley crew. There were only about thirty of them and a number of these were wearing only bits and pieces of army uniform. Some were bareheaded; two were in woollen caps and seamen's jerseys, one had plimsolls on his feet, while another was in wellingtons. All in all, he had never seen anything like it on a parade.

Strangely enough, the sergeant who had lined them up appeared to be quite unsurprised and started calling the roll as though nothing were amiss. Sterne was to learn later that the ill-clad men were survivors from a torpedoed ship and had lost all their kit. They were now waiting to be rekitted and sent home on leave.

The parade was pretty much of a mess in all respects. Reading from a clipboard, the sergeant called out the names, but several of those called were absent, apparently having already been embarked on some ship or other, while others were in fact present but not down on the list. It was obvious that the nominal roll was not being kept properly up to date, and Sterne got the impression that things were still very much in the process of being organised.

He had been there for two weeks, more or less killing time, when he was suddenly informed that he had been allotted a team of one lance-bombardier and four gunners, none of whom he had previously seen, and was to be embarked that day on board the S.S. *Dagon*. This also happened to be the day when the battery was to move its headquarters to Southport on the other side of the country and only one junior lieutenant had been left behind as a kind of rearguard to clear up any outstanding business.

Under his guidance they were transported on the back of an army truck to the naval depot where they were to draw their sea kit: hammocks, blankets, gumboots, oilskins and duffel-coats. In addition they were given a very basic civilian outfit of jacket, trousers and cloth cap for wear in any neutral ports to which they might go.

By the time all this gear had been collected it was well on into the afternoon, and they were now transported to a quay from which it was possible to see the S.S. *Dagon* moored between two other vessels some distance out in the river. A motor-launch was waiting at the foot of some very slippery-looking steps which might have been especially designed as a trap for hobnailed boots. And down those steps they were expected to carry all the kit that was piled up in the truck.

It was just not on. To the obvious disgust of the crusty and rather elderly man in charge of the launch, they began to drop the various items from the quay into the launch. One of the blankets missed its mark and fell into the water. It had to be fished out sopping wet, but the rest landed safely.

'Now,' the lieutenant said, 'down you go.'

They descended the steps gingerly. There was green weed clinging to the lower ones and water was lapping softly against the stonework. Sterne caught that odour which he was to come to know so well, of a great river flowing to the sea. It stirred something in him, a desire he had once had as a boy of becoming a sailor, enchanted by tales of Drake and Nelson. It had remained with him, suppressed, thrust into the background, but still not quite dead. Now it came alive again, and in this odd way that old desire was to be gratified: as a soldier he was to become a sailor, a soldier-sailor.

The launch carried them to the three moored ships, and here another problem had to be faced. To get to the *Dagon* they would have to board the ship nearest to the shore. This vessel, without cargo, stood high in the water, and the great steel hull rose like a sheer cliff with nothing but a Jacob's ladder dangling from the bulwarks to give access to the deck. A man could climb it, but not with the burden of his kit.

It was the lieutenant who pointed out the answer to the problem. 'Send two men up to find a rope. They can lower it and hoist the kit.'

It was the obvious thing to do. The boatman had certainly known it, but he was sullen and not saying a word. He was just holding the launch alongside the ship and watching the proceedings with a cynical eye.

Sterne told two of the men to climb aboard, and they went up the ladder rather clumsily. They reached the top and vanished from sight. Time passed and the lieutenant became impatient.

'Come with me, Bombardier. We'll go up and see what's what.'

They left the lance-bombardier to see to the kit and climbed the Jacob's ladder. When they reached the deck of the ship the two gunners who had preceded them were just returning with a length of rope which they had found. They lowered one end over the side and the kit-hoisting operation began.

'We'd better go and take a look at your ship, Bombardier,' the lieutenant said. 'This way.'

They crossed the deserted deck, the crew apparently being all ashore and nothing moving except a cat which came to see what was going on. A plank had been laid across the bulwarks to serve as a bridge between the two ships. Below it was a kind of iron-sided chasm at the bottom of which the dirty water was swilling around. The lieutenant walked across first with a nonchalance which might have been assumed, and Sterne followed, not looking down.

There was deck ballast on the *Dagon*, which was a three-island ship with well-decks fore and aft. The ballast looked like very poor slatey coal, and it had been dumped on the hatches and had dribbled down into the scuppers. Sterne had never imagined that ballast would be carried on deck; he would have expected it to be in the hold. But here it was; and very awkward it was to prove too.

'We'd better find the captain,' the lieutenant said. 'If he's aboard.'

The captain was. They found him in his cabin amidships. He was an elderly grey-haired man, who might possibly have been drawn out of retirement because of the emergency of war. His name was Wilson. The lieutenant introduced himself and Sterne.

'The bombardier and his detachment will be manning the Bofors gun.'

'But you know,' Wilson said, 'we don't sail for another four days. I wasn't expecting the gunners yet.'

'Force of circumstances, I'm afraid. Anyway, it'll give them time to settle in.'

'Yes, I suppose so. The cook and the steward won't be on board until morning. If they want some food I can maybe find something for them in the pantry.'

'That will be fine, Captain.'

They took leave of him and went to have a look at the gun, which was mounted on a steel platform above the poop and had to be reached by way of a vertical ladder. It had a low steel surround in which were lockers for the ready-use ammunition. The gun was under a canvas cover, and when they had removed this it was revealed to be in a pretty dirty condition in spite of having been partially protected from the weather. There was condensation on the metal and a little rust here and there. Some of the soot which seemed to have laid a coating on every part of the ship had managed to creep under the canvas and deposit itself on the metal.

'You'll have to get to work on this,' the lieutenant said. 'It's not had any care and maintenance lately.'

There was an old 4-inch breech-loading gun on the deck below, its barrel pointing over the stern. There were also two Hotchkiss machine-guns in boxes on each wing of the bridge, but none of these was Sterne's responsibility. The lieutenant told him that there was a DEMS leading seaman and two ratings to handle that part of the armament. In the unlikely event of the 4-inch being needed for defence against a U-boat or surface raider members of the crew would make up the required number to operate it.

They went next to inspect the quarters, which turned out to be a wooden hut erected at the after end of the boat-deck. In this small cabin were six bunks in two tiers, a hinged board attached to one side to serve as a table, a collapsable bench to sit on and a washstand. This was the home he, David Sterne, was to share with five other men, of whom he as yet knew practically nothing apart from their names, for a sea voyage of unpredictable duration.

Well, he had volunteered for it. There was a saying in the army: Never volunteer for anything. Perhaps there was reason in that.

*

Four days later the S.S. *Dagon* slipped down the Tyne and hit the swell of the North Sea. He was as sick as a toad, and it was little consolation to remember that Nelson was sick every time he went to sea. At least he had had a cabin to himself.

Chapter Fifteen – BALLAST

Three of the gunners were Scotsmen. Their names were McNab, Buchan and Douglas. Angus McNab was a tall, craggy, black-haired man. Rory Buchan was short and thick-set, with a pale complexion and prematurely white hair. Hamish Douglas was younger than the other two; a joker with red hair and a broad face.

The lance-bombardier came from Nottingham; his name was Joseph Carr. He was a quiet man, having little to say for himself. For a time Sterne thought he might be wise and intelligent but preferred to keep the wisdom locked away in his own head. Later he was forced to the conclusion that the head was pretty empty and that there was no wisdom to keep in it anyway. He wondered why the man had ever been given a stripe.

The fifth man was an East Anglian; he came from Norwich and his name was Albert Tuck. He was relatively old, being in his late thirties. He was also coarse, opinionated, unpleasant and thoroughly useless.

Not that any of them were much use when it came to the push, and Sterne had to resign himself to the fact that he had been dealt a bad hand. It was not altogether surprising; a lot of misfits had been weeded out of the light anti-aircraft batteries when the call had gone round for volunteers; it was only natural. He had had the misfortune to be landed with five of them. He wondered what Smith 124 was doing at that moment. He could have used a few men like him right now. But he would just have to make the best of what he had.

His seasickness passed fairly quickly and he was never to be bothered with it again. It had put him off smoking for a while, but when it had gone he went back to the cigarettes; they were free of excise duty when bought from the steward on board ship and consequently cheap to buy in tins of fifty. He smoked Capstan and sometimes State Express 777 or Senior Service. The old leading seaman, whose name was Gregg, rolled his own with cigarette tobacco that smelt like old rope burning.

They sailed up the east coast in a twin-column convoy of mixed coasters and deep-sea ships. The *Dagon* was a five thousand tonner and so old she seemed to be gradually turning to rust. Nobody bothered to scrape off the rust now; the universal grey paint was just slapped on top of it and after a while it came through again like a disease. The acrid smoke drifting back from the funnel had little pieces of grit in it. It caught at the throat and laid its quota of soot on the Bofors gun, which was uncovered and ready for action.

The convoy passed through the Pentland Firth by night and was attacked by a single German plane which they could hear but could not see. There was little response from the ships and the bombs all missed their target. The rest of the coastal voyage passed without incident.

Next day the S.S. *Dagon* anchored in Loch Ewe where an Atlantic convoy was being assembled. Leading Seaman Gregg, who was an old hand at the game, pointed out to Sterne the various types of ship gathered there in the shadow of the surrounding hills. There were some with the funnel near the stern and long catwalks connecting poop to bridge and bridge to forecastle.

'Hell-ships,' Gregg said.

He was a heavy, slightly stooping man with a deeply lined face. He had a full beard which was turning grey and a gunlayer's badge of crossed gun-barrels on his sleeve, together with the anchor which signified his rank.

'Hell-ships?' Sterne said.

'Tankers. You want to steer clear of them. They'll maybe carry ten thousand tons of high octane petrol. Get a tin fish in that lot and up she goes, a proper Brock's benefit. I've seen 'em. They set the sea alight. So my advice to you is, give 'em a wide berth.'

Sterne thought it was good advice, but the fact was that he would never be given the choice. If he was assigned to a tanker at any time in the future it would be useless to object. You had to take what came along.

*

There were forty merchant ships in the convoy that sailed from Loch Ewe when the anti-submarine nets at the entrance opened to let them pass. Once clear of the Western Isles they were formed up into eight columns, the destroyers and corvettes moving around them like collie dogs with a flock of sheep. In the middle was a larger ship, an armed merchant cruiser with six-inch guns for defence against surface raiders.

But this was destined to be a lucky convoy. The weather was good; no marauding Focke-Wulf Kurier found them and no U-boats attacked. Life for the gunners was uncomfortable in the cramped little hutch on the boat-deck, but comfort was hardly to be expected in the circumstances. Meals had to be fetched from the galley, which was if anything a degree filthier than the rest of the ship, and getting hot water for washing purposes entailed making a journey down several ladders to the engine-room in the bowels of the ship. Here the elderly reciprocating steam-engine did its work while the firemen in the stokehold fed the glowing furnace with coal and hoped no torpedo would suddenly smash its way through the hull.

But discomfort could be endured: the scrambling over the heaps of ballast, the climbing of swaying ladders, the watches on the gun in that narrow steel enclosure, the groping of one's way around the blacked-out ship in pitch-darkness – all this was of no account as long as the vessel stayed afloat. That was what really mattered; not to have salt water pouring in through a great jagged hole in the side, not to be immersed in that hungry sea which had swallowed ships and seamen without number and could never be surfeited.

*

So the days passed and there came a time when the chief mate came to the gunners with an offer from the captain. The ship was now nearing her destination, which was Montreal, and it was necessary to clear the ballast from the well-decks before entering the St Lawrence River. If the gunners cared to take on the job they would be paid one pound each for their labour.

Sterne put it to the men. They were no longer doing gun-watches, being out of range of any German plane, and the task for six strong men with shovels looked pretty simple. They were all willing.

Sterne went back to the mate. 'We'll do it, sir.'

The mate gave a smile, which might have meant anything, and went away to inform the captain.

'Easy money,' McNab said. 'We'll do the wee job in a day. Two at most.'

The shovels were supplied by the bosun and they set to work, beginning with the for'ard well-deck, three men on each side. It took Sterne less than an hour to reach the conclusion that, whatever else it might be, it was certainly not going to be easy money, and the job was not going to be done in a day.

The ballast was hellish stuff to tackle. There were large pieces and there were small pieces, and there was some that was little more than dust. It was difficult to get the shovels into it, and then the load had to be lifted over the bulwark and tipped into the sea. It was back-breaking work, hand-blistering work, to which none of them had been accustomed. And much of the ballast had to be shifted twice or even three times, since it was impossible to fling a shovelful directly from the hatch and over the bulwark; it had to be first tipped on to the deck and shovelled from there into the sea.

Leading Seaman Gregg came and looked at them with a grin on his face. 'Happy in your work?'

'What do you think?' Sterne said.

'I think you've been had. The Old Man got me on that job once. Never again. You know how it is? If he don't get rid of this ballast before we reach port he'll have to pay through the nose to have it cleared by a shore gang. At six quid for the job he's sitting pretty.'

'You could have told me this before we took it on.'

'You didn't ask me,' Gregg said.

Sterne thought about hitting him with the shovel, but thought better of it. It was not Gregg's fault that they had all misjudged the size of the job.

Tuck was in favour of their withdrawing from the contract. 'I vote we chuck it in. I've had enough.'

'No,' Sterne said. 'We agreed to do the job and we're not going to back out now.'

'I can't do any more. I've got a bad back and my hands are sore.'

'Ah, dinna be such a bloody milksop,' Buchan said. 'We'll do it. We said we would, and we will.'

The others seemed to agree with him, and Tuck, seeing himself in a minority of one, gave in with a bad grace. The work went on. At the end of the first day they had made some impression on the hill of ballast but there was still a lot left. Next morning they were all stiff in the joints, but the stiffness wore off as they continued with the work. The sun was hot on their backs and they were sweating freely. The dust stuck to their sweat.

The convoy dispersed, each ship going its own way, and the S.S. *Dagon* ploughed a lonely furrow westward, the course of her passage marked by splashes on either side as each successive shovelful of ballast was tipped overboard. From their position on the bridge the officers could gaze down upon the sweating galley slaves below, but what they were thinking it was impossible to guess.

*

It took three days to clear the for'ard well-deck; and then there was the one on the other side of the mid-castle that had to be tackled. They were still hard at it when the ship entered the estuary of the St Lawrence River. They had been shovelling hard for six days when the task was finally completed and the decks were free from the hated ballast.

'Three hundred and fifty tons,' Gregg said. 'That's what you've shifted. It'd have cost forty or fifty quid in Montreal. Over two hundred dollars. But I expect you're happy.'

'Yes, I am,' Sterne said. 'Happy it's finished.'

Chapter Sixteen – **HOMEWARD BOUND**

There was a heat-wave in Montreal; temperatures hitting ninety. The S.S. *Dagon* lay under the shadow of the monster silos and wheat poured into the holds in golden streams.

The dust from the wheat covered that other sooty layer which was always present, and it was so fine that it penetrated into the wooden cabin on the boat-deck and lay like a pale film on everything within. Wherever your fingers went you felt it; it stuck to the sweat on your face and got into the folds of your clothing and bedding; you breathed it in and tasted it on your tongue. While the grain poured into the holds the dust was something you had to live with.

Sterne went ashore and had scarcely got clear of the docks when a large American car drew up beside him and a fat bald-headed man who was at the wheel leaned out and addressed him.

'Hey, soldier, can you tell me which way I gotta go to get back to the United States? I've been drivin' all over and hell if I can find which road to take.'

'Sorry,' Sterne said. 'I've only just arrived from England. I'm a stranger here myself.'

The American stared at him. 'You kiddin'?'

'No kidding. And I'll tell you something else. It's going to be a lot harder for me to get back home than it is for you.'

'Sonuvabitch!' the man said, and drove off.

He took a sightseeing tour round the city and suburbs on the upper deck of an open-topped tramcar. The Frenchness of it was apparent everywhere; all the street signs were in the two languages, and he heard people speaking French for the first time since he had left France by way of the beach at Malo-les-Bains.

He went into a stationer's shop to buy a notebook. The assistant spoke English and brought up the subject of the effect of the War on the Canadian economy.

'Everything's going up in price. Take Coke. I used to pay five cents for a bottle; now it's six.'

'Is that so?' Sterne said.

He could see how war in Europe was beginning to bite even here in Montreal. But life had to go on, whatever the price of Coke.

*

One day a Canadian official of some kind came on board. The mate introduced him to Sterne and said that the man had a wish to take a look at the Bofors gun, if that was all right.

Sterne could see no reason why it should not be all right. The man looked perfectly harmless and he was hardly likely to be a spy trying to obtain the secrets of the armament carried by British merchant ships.

So they climbed the ladders to the poop and the gun enclosure, and Sterne explained the working of the mechanism and the method of loading and firing, all of which the visitor seemed to find quite fascinating and would probably tell his wife when he got home. When they returned to the mid-castle he pointed at some jagged holes in the ship's funnel.

'Enemy action?'

Sterne did not deny it. Why spoil a good story by telling the plain truth, which was that the holes had been caused by nothing more exciting than common rust? And that the entire ship was gradually disintegrating under the effect of this insidious disease.

Before leaving the man gave him a five-dollar bill for his trouble. He had slaved six days on the ballast to earn just that amount. Now he got it for a few minutes of his time and a slight lack of honesty regarding the ship's funnel. That was life.

*

They were there for three days. Then, with the wheat levelled off in the holds on either side of the central shifting-boards, the hatches were covered and the tarpaulins battoned down and the wedges driven home. Then the derrick booms were lowered into their cradles and the ship, with provisions for the voyage taken on board and the fresh-water tanks replenished, was ready to depart.

Unfortunately from Bombardier Sterne's point of view, when the time for departure next day was fast approaching it became evident that one of his men was missing. Hamish Douglas had been ashore all night and had not yet returned. Angus McNab had also spent the night ashore, but he had come back on board early in the morning looking rather the worse for wear and with the smell of alcohol on his breath.

The minutes ticked away and still no Douglas appeared. Sterne decided that Captain Wilson would have to be informed; there was nothing else for it. It was not a revelation he cared to make, but it had to be done. As might have been expected, the Old Man was not at all pleased.

'And you don't know where he is?'

'No, sir.'

'This is a bad business, a very bad business. You must understand we cannot wait. We have to leave on time. If he is not here by then we shall have to sail without him.'

'I realise that, sir.'

'And you'll be short of a man on the gun.'

Sterne thought of telling him that this would be no great loss; that Douglas was a useless bastard who had flogged his sea-boots and duffel-coat for beer money in a Tyneside pub before the ship left port in England, and that he had probably flogged more of his gear in Montreal. But there would have been no point in it.

He left the bridge and encountered McNab, who had a suggestion to make.

'I could gang ashore and fetch wee Hamish.'

'You know where he is?'

'Och aye. He'll be in the whore-house he's been spending his time in wi' the women.'

Sterne gave him a sharp glance. 'Is that where you've been too?'

McNab gave a sheepish grin. 'Some of the time.'

'And you're asking me to let you go and pick him up?'

'So I am.'

Sterne thought about it for two seconds and dismissed the idea. If he let McNab go he might end up with two men missing.

'No,' he said. 'You stay here.'

McNab shrugged. 'It's your say-so.'

*

The S.S. *Dagon* left Montreal without Hamish Douglas. Under the guidance of the river pilot they slipped downstream towards Quebec; but before they got as far as that a Norwegian ship overtook and passed them, moving pretty fast. The river was very wide at this point and the ship was some distance away.

'There's somebody in a hurry,' the gunlayer said. He was standing with Sterne on the poop. 'I've never seen that happen before. And there's no point in it anyway. We'll all be in the same convoy going home.'

It was not until they anchored off Quebec to change the pilot that the reason for the manoeuvre became apparent. A police launch came out from the shore, and when it drew near they could see standing in the cockpit the missing gunner, Hamish Douglas. He was bareheaded and wearing nothing but a shirt and trousers. When the launch came alongside he climbed on board, grinning sheepishly but not in the least repentant for the trouble he had caused.

It appeared that the Montreal police, alerted by Captain Wilson, had picked him up from the house in the red light district and had put him on board the Norwegian ship that was about to depart soon after the S.S. *Dagon*. The Norwegian, a fairly modern vessel, had a good turn of speed and had no difficulty in overtaking the aging British one. It had arrived at Quebec almost half an hour earlier.

'I waved to you as we went by,' Douglas said. 'Did ye not see me?'

Sterne had in fact seen someone waving but had thought it was one of the other ship's crew; at that distance it had been impossible to recognise the Scot. Now he told Douglas what he had refrained from telling the captain.

'You're a bloody useless bugger, Hamish. And you're a stupid bugger too. You know you could face a court-martial for this when we get back to England?'

Douglas seemed not at all put out. 'Och, there's no harm done, is there?'

'No thanks to you. And there's another thing: you're going to have to pay for all that kit you've flogged. There'll be a kit inspection when we get back and you'll need a good excuse to explain where it all went.'

Douglas gave a shrug. 'So mebbe I'll no be getting hame.'

There was always that, Sterne thought. But it was not something you liked to dwell on too much.

*

Quebec and the Plains of Abraham where long ago General Wolfe and a British army had defeated the French under Montcalm, were left astern and they proceeded downriver and into the Gulf of St Lawrence, the weather still hot and sultry. A convoy was assembling off Sydney in Cape Breton Island, and they joined it for the long voyage home, loaded with wheat and much lower in the water than they had been on the outward run.

Captain Wilson had left it to Sterne to deal with Douglas as he thought fit, and he had not yet made up his mind whether or not to report the incident when they rejoined the battery in Southport. It would cause a lot of bother for him as well as the gunner, and he wondered whether it was really worth it. Would it not be better to forget the whole thing? Perhaps.

The S.S. *Dagon* was in the middle of the extreme starboard column of the convoy. Leading Seaman Gregg, who always tended to look on the gloomy side of things, said it was not a good position.

'They can pick you off too easily.'

'Well, let's hope it won't come to that.'

'Ah, let's hope. That's what we live on. Hope.'

The entire convoy changed direction at regular intervals, zig-zagging its way across the Atlantic. Some sea-captains maintained that this was a useless manoeuvre and simply lost valuable time by lengthening the distance travelled, but the weight of opinion was against them. One thing was certain: it was not easy to keep the ships in position when all this zig-zagging was taking place. And there were always stragglers to be taken care of and those which went romping on ahead. The S.S. *Dagon* was continually being admonished by Aldis lamp or loud-hailer for making too much smoke. Smoke from a convoy could be seen for many miles and give away its position to searching U-boats. But how did you keep the speed of an old tub like this one up to the necessary rate of knots without making smoke?

For the North Atlantic the weather was passably good, and the convoy progressed without incident for the first week or so. For the gunners there was one improvement which they themselves had made: no ballast on the after well-deck impeded their journey from cabin to gun; it was now simply a matter of descending two ladders, crossing the deck and climbing two more ladders. On a fine day it was not unpleasant to stand in that little enclosure on its tall steel column and survey this portion of the world that lay within the limits of the great circle of the horizon. You came to know each individual ship in the convoy by sight, though those on the far side were small and indistinct except when viewed through binoculars. You had the feeling of being a member of a family; a family of nomads, forever on the move.

Sterne remarked to Leading Seaman Gregg that things were very quiet.

'Where have all the U-boats gone?'

The gunlayer sucked his breath in sharply. 'Don't ask. Don't even think about it.'

It was as though simply mentioning such things might bring them swarming round the convoy. Sterne knew that sailors were a superstitious lot. Nobody whistled in a ship. Maybe Gregg believed that a word could bring bad luck.

'We've got near two thousand miles still to go,' he said. 'And we're coming to the bad part.'

Sterne thought he was being pessimistic. There had not been any trouble on the voyage out, so why should there be any on the homeward run? He looked at the gently heaving sea around them and found it hard to imagine that any killer could be lurking beneath the surface. Yet reason told him that it was all too possible. The number of ships that had already been lost in convoys proved it. But maybe they would be lucky again.

Two days later he knew that they would not.

Chapter Seventeen – RESCUE

It happened late in the night, at two a.m. by the clock or four bells in the middle watch. Douglas and Carr had that watch on the gun, while the other four were asleep in the cabin.

There was no warning. The U-boat had approached undetected or had possibly been lying in wait with engines stopped for the convoy to move into position for the attack. The torpedo struck just forward of the poop.

Sterne was awakened by the blast and the shaking of the cabin. For a moment he was too confused to realise just what was happening. Was it a dream, a nightmare? The moment passed, his brain cleared, and he knew that this was no dream but stark reality. The cabin was not in complete darkness; there was a small blue bulb that was kept on all night, and he could see the other three men who had been wrenched from their sleep and were sitting up in their bunks. They all started talking at once, asking the same question.

'What happened? What was it?'

Sterne provided the answer that should have been obvious to all of them. 'We've been hit.' He spoke sharply, suppressing his own fear and putting a clamp on the panic that might have taken hold if given half a chance. 'Get dressed. Move it, move it.'

They were all out of their bunks now, reaching for clothes, pulling trousers on, knocking against one another in that confined space, the deck beginning to tilt under their feet.

Tuck was swearing. 'We're sinking. The bloody ship's going down!' His voice rose hysterically.

Sterne gripped his arm fiercely. 'Stow it!'

They could hear the ship's whistle going now. It was like the cry of a mortally wounded animal shuddering into the night, and it was the signal to leave. It jarred on frayed nerves, screaming at them as if to emphasise the extremity of the situation and the need for haste.

Sterne pulled his trousers on, tucking in the shirt he had been wearing, supporting his back against a bunk, slipping the braces over his shoulders.

He looked for sea-boots and could not find them. Someone staggered into him; it was McNab. He was muttering over and over like a refrain:

'Here's a carry-on, here's a carry-on, here's a carry-on.'

He clutched Sterne to hold himself up, but Sterne pushed him off.

'Get away from me. Get your life-jacket on. Move, damn you.'

He reached for his own kapok-padded jacket and slipped it on, not wasting time in fastening the tapes.

'Let's go! Let's go!'

They were still milling around in confusion. The deck under their feet was sloping more acutely. He began pushing them towards the door, using brute force as an aid to exhortation.

'Go, go, go! Boat stations! Go!'

There was a heavy canvas blackout curtain screening the door. Someone pulled it aside and pushed the door open. As they went out the warm fug of the cabin gave way to the fresh cold air of the night. A crescent moon, like a thin slice of melon, was hanging in the sky and giving a little pale light to the scene. Already some of the crew were at the boats which, as was the rule at sea, were hanging from their davits in the outboard position ready for lowering as soon as the gripes that secured them were released.

Sterne's boat station was on the port side, and he went to it immediately to give a hand with the falls as he had been instructed to do during boat-drill. McNab was with him, still muttering under his breath:

'Here's a carry-on! Here's a carry-on!'

Glancing aft, Sterne saw how much lower the after-castle was than normal. There was no doubt that the stern of the ship was going down, and there was water flowing across the well-deck, the ghostly pallor of the froth showing through the gloom. He could just make out the gun platform, which was leaning away from him now, and he wondered whether Douglas and Carr had been able to make it to the bridge-deck before the sea came surging across and cut them off. If not, they would have to trust to one of the rafts which were mounted on steel slides, one on each side of the poop. These could be launched with one blow of the hammer hanging on the mounting. But suppose they had been caught in that rush of water as they tried to cross the well-deck. He banished the thought from his mind, having more pressing matters to think about.

The third mate, who was in command of the boat, arrived. Under his orders they began to lower away. The slope of the deck made it difficult to keep the boat level. There were two men in it, and they were almost tipped out as it hit the water stern first. It levelled and began to bounce on the swell, banging against the side of the ship.

'Get aboard now,' the third mate said. 'Smartly.'

The rest of the party slid down the ropes and into the boat. The third mate followed them.

'Release the falls.'

The falls were unhooked and the boat floated free. Two men pushed it away from the side of the ship with oars. Others took up oars, Sterne among them, and began to pull away from the ship, which was now going down more and more by the stern.

She had lost way and the ships that had been astern of her were passing her by and ploughing on. Soon she had dropped completely out of the convoy. They stopped rowing and rested on the oars. Sterne gazed ahead at the dark shapes of those other ships going steadily away from them and had a feeling of being abandoned. There was another boat not far away, but he could see nothing of those which had been on the other side of the ship, nor could he see any raft which might have come from the poop.

His gaze returned to the receding convoy and as he watched suddenly a great column of fire shot up into the sky, followed by the dull rumble of the explosion.

'Jesus Christ!' one of the seamen said. 'There's a bloody tanker's bought it.'

So the U-boat had struck again, or it might have been a different one. Maybe there was a pack of them. He thought about what Leading Seaman Gregg had said respecting tankers. He had called them hell-ships; and it looked as if some people were going through a very nasty piece of hell at that very moment.

He wondered whether Gregg had got away safely, and if so whether he would be blaming all this on those incautious words he, Sterne, had spoken two days ago. Gregg had told him that he had been on board the old *Dagon* almost from the start of the War, and he had seen plenty of ships go down, but this one had borne a charmed life. Now that happy state of affairs had come to an end with the very first voyage that a certain Bombardier David Sterne had made in her. So was he a Jonah? Maybe Gregg would think so, but of course it would be nothing but superstition: the ship would have suffered precisely the same fate if he had never set foot on board.

She was going down rapidly now; the poop was almost submerged. The bows, in a kind of seesaw movement, were actually rising. But it would not save them; the stern would go down and drag everything else with it. And a few minutes later it happened: the rusty old ship had come to the end of her life and was taking her cargo of wheat with her to the bed of the ocean, leaving on the surface only a scattering of flotsam that was scarcely visible from the boat.

The fire continued to burn in the distance. For a time it revealed the black shapes of the other ships, but they moved on and left it. And then suddenly the column of red flame vanished like a candle snuffed out.

'She's gone,' the seaman said.

But a few smaller fires continued to burn, spread over a wider area, and Sterne concluded that this was petrol burning on the surface. And there were perhaps men struggling in that inferno. What hope for them?

Very soon these fires died away too, and the convoy had gone from their view. Sterne shivered. There was a light breeze blowing and he felt the chill of it through his shirt. He wished he had put on his duffel-coat before leaving the cabin; there would probably have been time. But in the confusion the overriding thought had been to get away, not to be trapped in the cabin. There were a dozen men in the boat, sitting on the thwarts, not talking much, shocked, trying to come to terms with the situation. The second engineer was the only officer there besides the third mate. The black donkeyman and the carpenter were also present. The rest were seamen and firemen, one of whom must have come straight up from the stokehold and was wearing nothing but a singlet and thin cotton trousers. He must have been feeling the cold even more, Sterne thought, having been sweating below decks before this sudden exposure to the elements.

McNab was sitting next to Sterne, hunched forward, hands on knees. He said:

'This is a fine old how-d'ye-do, Bom.'

'Well, you volunteered for it, same as me.'

'Aye, so I did. But I never thought it would come to this.'

Sterne was thinking again of that old soldier's dictum: 'Never volunteer for anything in the army.' He had ignored it and this was the result: adrift in a boat in the middle of the night and a thousand miles and more from land.

'You know what we are, Angus?'

'No,' McNab said. 'Tell me.'

'We're two bloody fools, that's what.'

'Aye,' McNab said. 'Either that or bloody heroes.'

'Do you feel like a hero, Angus?'

McNab shook his head. 'Just now I feel like a man that could do wi' a wee dram o' gude Scotch whisky.'

'You'd have to go a long way for that, I'm afraid.'

'Aye,' McNab said. And he gave a sigh.

He had once told Sterne that he came from a small town on the east coast of Scotland where his wife kept what he called a wee sweetie shop. It appeared that she sent him postal orders now and then to augment his army pay. He himself before the War had done 'this and that', from which Sterne gathered that he had been an odd job man, probably subsidised by Mrs McNab's sweetie shop.

Sterne had never disliked McNab; his only complaint against the man being that he was a bad gunner. Now he felt closer to him, and not only in the physical sense, than he had ever done before. It was as though adversity and a shared danger had drawn them together as comrades. Yet he knew that if the two of them survived he would make very sure that he never again went to sea with Angus McNab as one of his detachment. And that applied also to the rest of the team.

They were fortunate. They had been in the boat only a short time when the rescue ship found them, homing in on the light they were showing. The rescue ship was a small fast passenger vessel that in more peaceful times had carried out less hazardous duties for one of the Scottish coastal lines. Now, manned entirely by merchant seamen, it was performing one of the most dangerous of jobs, staying behind to pick up survivors while the rest of the convoy and escort moved on. It was a sitting duck for any U-boat that might have remained in the vicinity, since it was necessary to heave to while men were being taken up from boats or the water.

This ship took on board survivors from all the *Dagon*'s boats, but neither Douglas nor Carr was among them.

Sterne reflected that circumstances had conspired to render it unnecessary for him to report Gunner Hamish Douglas for his conduct in Montreal. Douglas would never face a court martial and never be forced to pay for the flogged items of kit. He had gone beyond the reach of military law.

Bombardier David Sterne found it impossible to gain any satisfaction whatever from this reflection.

Chapter Eighteen – FORTY-SECOND STREET

About a year later Sterne was in New York. He was now assigned to a freighter of six thousand tons called the *Northern Light*, a motor vessel powered by diesels. This was a relatively modern ship that had been built in a Birkenhead yard shortly before the outbreak of hostilities. The Bofors gun was mounted amidships, abaft the bridge, and the gunners' quarters were a few decks below in one large cabin just above the engine-room. While you were at sea you could hear the thump-thump-thump of the diesels going on and on and on. You got so used to it that it even lulled you to sleep. Not that gunners ever found it difficult to sleep even in the worst of conditions; the difficulty was in waking them to go on watch.

Sterne had had the same team now for three voyages, all in different ships. They had been to Bermuda and Jamaica and Argentina with no glimpse of a U-boat or a Focke-Wulf, and he had come to the conclusion that he was not a Jonah after all. The gunners were all new men, and he was well satisfied with them. Two of them had come to him straight from training camp. One of these, Dick Farman, had been a stevedore in the London docks. He was a tall lean man, rather older than Sterne, who did a lot of reading and was something of a hypochondriac. The other, Frank Lancaster, of about the same age, had been a printer in Watford. One of the others was very young; he had been in the first batch of conscripts called up in April 1939. His name was Danny Wicks, and he had the finest crop of pimples Sterne had ever seen. The other two were Liverpool men. John Staples had been a clerk in the office of one of the football pools firms and was a very precise and clerkly sort of person. The fifth man, Harry Carter, had been a tailor and would always oblige if a bit of sewing needed to be done.

Sterne felt himself fortunate to have these five men under his command. They made a good team and there was hardly ever any serious friction between them.

He had started writing again. He wrote short stories and verse and was currently working on a novel, which he was putting together in exercise books purchased in various ports of call. He had been engaged on the novel off and on for quite a while, carrying the manuscript about with him from ship to ship. Sometimes he thought it was pretty good; at other times he felt sure it was sheer rubbish and had best be thrown away. But he did not throw it away, and it gradually grew and took shape.

He read a lot. Most ships had small libraries, though the choice of books was limited. In New York they received stacks of old copies of *Time* and *Life* and other journals, and he discovered that American magazines and newspapers were very much fatter than their paper-starved British counterparts. He was particularly interested in the stories in *Saturday Evening Post* and *Atlantic* and *Collier's*, and wished he could have written something half as good.

The *Northern Light* had been delayed in New York for essential repairs to be carried out, a circumstance which Sterne and his team could not have found more to their liking. For servicemen in uniform New York was a delight. There was so much to see, so much to do. There were all sorts of institutions where free meals were provided, and free tickets were available for cinemas and theatres. There was no reason why anyone should want to leave the place and get to sea again.

*

One day he went ashore with Dick Farman and they found themselves walking down 42nd Street.

'Do you remember,' he said 'a film called *Forty-Second Street*?'

Farman did remember it. 'All dancing and singing. Lots of lovely girls. I saw it three times. All them legs! Cor!'

Sterne remembered it too. It had been one of those backstage spectaculars, with crowds of dancers going through the glittering routines and singers belting out the songs. It had been the time of the big Hollywood musicals: *Broadway, Broadway Melody, Gold Diggers of Broadway*. Stars like Joan Blondell, Ruby Keeler, Dick Powell and Warner Baxter were in them. The depression was hitting America hard; in 1929 the Wall Street crash had ruined vast numbers of stock market speculators – and in those days half the population was speculating. The cinema was a way of escape from all that; a place where for a few hours you could sink into a plush seat amid luxurious surroundings and live in another world.

'They were gorgeous,' Farman said.

But somehow this 42nd Street was not much like the one in the film; it was too ordinary, too drab even. But of course the film had been the Hollywood idea of the street; it had been a view of it from a couple of thousand miles away. Still, the street had something now that the film had never had: it had the Stage Door Canteen. And in there you not only got free grub, you had it served by people from the New York stage, and maybe had a few cabaret turns thrown in.

Sterne had been there before, but Farman had not. He was quick to agree to the suggestion that they should go inside.

'You think we'll see some stars?'

'Probably nobody you'll recognise. These are stage people, not film actors. You won't find Marlene Dietrich or Loretta Young here.'

They went in through the rather unimpressive entrance and left their caps and greatcoats with the cloakroom girl, receiving a numbered tag in exchange. Beyond the entrance lobby there was a large room with a lot of tables and on the left a dais or stage with wooden railings round it. There was music being played by a juke-box, and in the enclosure a couple of American soldiers and a sailor were jitterbugging with three girls in tight roll-neck sweaters and flared skirts.

They found a table and a waitress in a red, white and blue striped apron came across to take their orders. She glanced at their uniforms and said:

'Oh, you're English, aren't you?' Then she took a closer look at Sterne and said: 'Oh, my God! David!'

It was as much of a surprise to him as it was to her. He could hardly believe what he was seeing.

'Angela! But it's not possible. What on earth are you doing here?'

'It's obvious, isn't it?' she said. 'I'm doing my stint of waiting on the troops. Don't look so amazed. I'm in a show.'

'On Broadway?'

'Yes, on Broadway.'

'But how –'

'Oh,' she said, 'it's far too long a story to tell just now. And anyway, if it comes to that, what are you doing here yourself?'

'I'm from a ship. We're in dock at the moment.'

'But you're not a sailor. Not in that uniform.'

'I'm a soldier-sailor.' He showed her the shoulder badge of fouled anchor and the letters R.A. 'Maritime Royal Artillery. We man anti-aircraft guns on merchant ships.'

'Oh, I see.'

Farman was staring wide-eyed during this exchange. Now he broke in with a question that could hardly have been more superfluous, the answer being self-evident.

'You two know each other?'

Angela treated him to one of her most dazzling smiles. 'However did you guess?'

'From way back,' Sterne said.

They looked at each other in silence for a moment or two. There was so much to say, such a vast gap to fill. But it could not be said there. They both seemed to realise this and were momentarily tongue-tied.

Then she said: 'Look, I've got this job to do. You'd better give me your orders.'

Sterne laughed. 'That's very professional of you.' and into his mind there came the memory of a day long ago when they had first lunched together in a Lyons teashop and had been served by a Nippie in a black dress and a frilly white cap. He wondered whether she would remember if he reminded her. But he did not put it to the test.

When she had gone to fetch their order Farman said: 'Now that really is one lovely girl. How'd you ever get to know her?'

'Wouldn't you just like to know?'

'Yes. But you're not going to tell me, are you?'

'Not now. Not here.'

He doubted whether he would ever tell it. Not the whole of it certainly. It was not something he wished to share with anyone.

She came back with a tray and set out the things on the table, doing it with the dainty elegant movements that were natural to her and which he remembered so well and with a poignant longing.

She said to him: 'We've got to talk, but it's impossible here. We must meet somewhere. How long will you be in New York?'

'I don't know. Not long. A few more days maybe.'

They had already been there a week. A wasted week, he realised now. If only they had met earlier. If only he had known she was there.

'Tomorrow,' she said. 'What are you doing tomorrow?'

'Nothing important.'

'Could you meet me at, say, one o'clock?'

'I think it could be managed.'

He would make damned sure it could. He would have moved heaven and earth to see her again.

She found a card and wrote on it. 'This is my address. You can find your way?'

'You bet.'

She looked at him again, her head tilted slightly. 'You're older.'

'It's what happens. The years pass.'

He thought she looked older too, more mature. But this maturity had if anything made her even more beautiful.

'Oh, my darling,' she said, with a little catch in her voice, 'it's so good to see you again.'

And then she stooped quickly and kissed him on the lips and was gone.

'She called you darling,' Farman said. It was like an accusation.

'It was nothing. Stage people; they call everybody darling.'

'Not like that. She called you her darling. She kissed you too.'

'Oh,' Sterne said, 'you noticed.'

'She didn't kiss me.' Farman sounded faintly aggrieved.

'I'm sure it was just an oversight.'

'And she wants you to meet her tomorrow. Know what I think?'

'No. What do you think?'

'I think you're a bloody lucky sod,' Farman said.

Chapter Nineteen – TAKE CARE

It was an apartment on the second floor of an old brownstone house some way from the stir and bustle of Broadway. The names of the occupants were listed with a row of push-buttons at one side of the doorway. He pressed the button allotted to A. L. Street and heard a click and then a voice coming from the grille.

'Who is it?'

'It's me,' he said. 'David.'

'Oh, fine, come on up.'

He heard the mechanism working to unlock the door, and he went into the lobby and up the stairs, and she was waiting for him in the doorway of her apartment.

'Come in,' she said. 'Do come in.'

He went in and she closed the door and locked it. And then they were in each other's arms in an instant without saying another word, as if some irresistible magnetic force had drawn them together.

*

They stayed in the apartment until it was time for her to leave for the theatre. They had a meal and made love and talked and talked. The apartment was not large, but it had everything one could have asked for to make living easy. There was only one bedroom, but the bed was all that could have been desired. He looked for a sign of any other male having been there, but he could find none. This pleased him.

There came a time when he could no longer resist asking the question that was floating in his mind.

'What happened to Judas?'

'We split up.'

'Ah!'

She hesitated for a few moments. Then: 'Okay; I'd better tell you. It was all a mistake; it didn't take me long to realise that. It was the most God-awful mistake I've ever made. He just wasn't the man I remembered. Maybe prison changed him; made him harder, meaner; maybe that's what being inside does to a man, I don't know. All I know is that I wasn't in love with him any more. Perhaps it was because I was still in love with you.'

'With me!'

'Does it surprise you so very much?'

'But you left me. You went to him.'

'Yes, I know, damn it. But all the time I had this feeling that I was taking the wrong step. And you didn't help.'

'How could I have helped?'

'You gave in too easily. You should have fought for me, argued with me, refused to let me go. But you didn't, and I got the idea that you didn't care, that you didn't really want me all that much.'

'My God!' he said. 'How could you believe that?'

'Wasn't it true?'

'Of course it wasn't. It nearly drove me out of my mind, your leaving. It was like the end of the world for me.'

But he could see that she was right; he hadn't fought hard enough. He had let her go too easily. Maybe he had deserved to lose her.

'I'm sorry,' she said. 'I didn't want to hurt you. And I was really afraid of what Jude might do.'

'But then you left him?'

'Yes.'

'Didn't he put up a fight?'

'No. I think all he really wanted was to get me away from you. It was his pride. He resented you taking me from him. His property, as he saw it. But once he'd done it he didn't care any more. We had a flaming row, and that was that.'

'Why didn't you come back to me?'

'Pride again, I suppose. How could I? I thought about it. Believe me, I really did think about it; but I couldn't bring myself to do it.'

They were both silent for a while, thinking back in time. Thinking of what might have been.

'So after that,' Sterne said. 'After you'd split up, what then?'

'Nothing for a bit. Then I auditioned for a new musical called *Up, Up and Away*. I thought it might just be in the chorus, but they seemed to like me and I got one of the supporting roles. Then there was this American producer who planned to put the show on on Broadway. He had a look at the London production, and I must have made an impression on him because he came round backstage and invited me to go to New York and join the American company. The money he was offering was too good to refuse, and he made it okay with the London management and in a few days there I was on board the *Queen Mary* on my way to the States.'

'Just like a fairy tale.'

'Wasn't it? But the show never took wings on Broadway. Perhaps it was too English. It ran for a few weeks, then died. By this time war had broken out in Europe and I stayed on. The producer was putting on another musical at another theatre and he gave me a part. *Let's Go* has been running ever since.'

The producer's name was Henry Hanks. Sterne wondered whether there had been anything going between her and Hanks that might have influenced him when it came to giving this lift to her stage career. That sort of thing happened, so he had heard. The Hollywood casting couch was notorious. But he dismissed the thought as unworthy. Why should she not have been taken for her talent alone? He knew she had plenty.

'So,' she said, 'that's me brought up to date. Now what about you? How did you come to be a soldier-sailor?'

He told her. He told her about Dunkirk and about the sinking of his first ship.

'Oh, David,' she said; and he could tell how concerned she was for his safety. 'Why did you have to go and put your neck in it?'

'That's a good question,' he said. But he gave no answer to it. Perhaps he did not know the answer himself.

She asked about the Lakoses. 'How are they getting on?'

'You didn't hear?'

'Hear what?'

'They were arrested. They'd been passing secret information to the Germans from a transmitter in the attic. The bookshop was just a front, a meeting-place for spies.'

She was amazed. 'I can't believe it. They were such a nice couple. I liked them.'

'So did I. But you never know, do you?'

She was silent for a few moments, evidently turning this revelation over in her mind and feeling pretty sad about it. Then she said:

'How about the writing? I don't suppose you get the chance to do any these days.'

'Oh yes,' he said. 'You'd be surprised. There are long hours of utter boredom at sea when nothing much is happening and you're not on watch or doing chores. Of course you're always aware that a torpedo could come bursting in on you at any moment, but you can't be thinking about that all the time. You'd go crazy.'

'It must be terrible,' she said; and she gave a little shudder.

'Ah, it's not so bad. I'd rather be in a ship than in a submarine. In one of those tin cans life must be hell.'

'And so you are writing. What are you on now?'

'Well, I've started a novel.'

'Oh, lovely. How's it going?'

'By fits and starts. I carry it around with me and add to it whenever I get the chance.'

'Is it good? Oh, but it must be.'

'I'm not so sure.'

'Well, I am,' she said. 'I believe in you. I always have.'

Which was nice to know.

*

One evening he went to see *Let's Go*. Angela gave him a ticket. He enjoyed the show and thought she was splendid. He could tell that she was a favourite with the audience, and he could see why. She was delightful, and he had not realised that she could sing so well. Hers was not the chief part but it was an important one, and her name was up in lights. She was obviously on the way up, and it depressed him a little, because he wondered whether he would ever be able to keep pace with her. But he was glad for her sake.

He went to her dressing-room after the final curtain. She was sitting in front of a mirror and cleaning up, but she turned and gave him a kiss. He caught the mingled odour of sweat and grease-paint and powder, and it excited him. It was so powerfully sensual.

'So what did you think of it, darling?'

'I loved it. You were marvellous. I never dreamed you could be so good.'

'Ah,' she said, 'you would say that, wouldn't you?'

But he could see that she was pleased.

'I don't need to say it. The audience must tell you. You had them eating out of your hand. Is it always like this?'

'There are good nights and not so good nights. But mostly they're good.'

He had something to tell her now, and he wondered how she would take it. He hated the necessity, but he had no choice.

'This is the last time I shall see you – for the present. Some other time perhaps. Who knows?'

She stared at him and seemed to go rigid. 'What are you saying?'

'We sail tomorrow. Shore leave ends at midnight.'

'Oh no!' It was like a wail of anguish. 'Not so soon.'

'Yes, so soon.'

'Then we must go to my place. We must hurry.'

He shook his head. 'There's no time. I couldn't get back to the ship before the deadline. I must say goodbye to you here.' He glanced at his wrist-watch. 'I'm driving it pretty close as it is.'

She stood up, pushing the chair away from her. 'Then we must do it here. Lock the door.'

He did so, and when he turned he saw that her dressing-gown was lying on the floor and she was kicking off her shoes.

'Hurry, David, hurry!'

Someone knocked on the door. 'Miss Street! Are you in there?'

'Go away!' she screamed. 'Go away, go away!'

Whoever it was went away and left them to themselves.

They acted with a kind of desperate frenzy, as though they both knew it might be the last time ever between them. For tomorrow a ship would slip down-river to that wide dark lethal sea where the U-boats lurked, and he would be in that ship. And there was nothing that she could do to protect him, except maybe pray. And what good would that do? What good at all?

'I love you, David,' she whispered. 'Oh God, I love you so much. Why do you have to go?' She wept and the tears ran down her face and streaked it with mascara. 'Why, why, why?'

And when he was leaving she kissed him for the last time, and wiped her eyes and said:

'Take care of yourself, my darling.'

And he promised he would, and knew that no amount of taking care would help him if his time had come, because that was the way of things.

Chapter Twenty – LIFE IS SWEET

He was in the water and the life-jacket was all that was keeping him afloat. It had all happened so suddenly. The torpedo must have struck amidships. It was the middle of the night and he had been on watch with Danny Wicks. He had heard a great roar beneath him and Danny giving a cry, and then he was flying through the air, caught in some upward blast that flung him clear of the ship and dumped him in the sea.

The shock of immersion in the chilly water cleared his brain, and he realised what had happened. He realised too that something was wrong with his right arm; it was hurting like hell and he was unable to use it. It did not occur to him for the moment that it might be broken; that realisation was to come later, but for the present he was aware only of the pain.

The superstructure of the ship loomed above him, and he had a fear that if it toppled over on that side it would fall on him and thrust him under. He made a desperate effort to swim away from it, but the right arm was useless and he was hampered by the duffel-coat he was wearing under the life-jacket.

He could see nothing of Danny Wicks, and indeed he was never to see the kid again; nor any of the rest of his men, because they had been asleep in the cabin above the engine-room and that was where the torpedo had struck. They had stood no chance of survival.

Now he noticed that the ship was moving away from him. It had been going forward at a rate of maybe seven knots when it had been torpedoed, and though the engines were immediately put out of action, the momentum of the six thousand ton ship was carrying it on. It had been the last ship in the convoy on the starboard side and Sterne himself was now being left behind by all the vessels.

He felt sure the *Northern Light* would not take long to sink; its cargo of tanks and guns and trucks would ensure that once the water came pouring in the end would not be long in coming. He could not tell whether any of the lifeboats had been launched; it was possible that they had been damaged by the explosion and rendered useless. Very soon he had lost sight of the vessel; it had vanished into the darkness, as had the other ships. He heard a distant explosion and saw a flicker of light far ahead, which could only mean that another ship had been torpedoed. But that was far away from where he floated like a human buoy with the little red battery light clipped to the shoulder of the life-jacket shining dimly through the gloom. He had switched it on with only the faintest hope that it might be seen. But by whom? It was so small, a mere pinpoint in a vast expanse of heaving ocean.

Suddenly he heard gunfire from the direction of the convoy, and starshells were going up, revealing the dark outlines of the ships, small in the distance. He guessed that a U-boat had been discovered on the surface and some of the warships were firing at it. But his interest in this was minimal. It was not his affair any more; he was out of it, left behind. He could taste the salt on his tongue and feel the pain in his arm and had a terrible sense of having been abandoned. He was so completely alone. Could there be a worse loneliness than this? Floating with his head just above the water and all around him this heaving waste that was home only to the cold-blooded creatures that were born in it. He had a feeling that this was it; this was the last farewell; he was finished.

But he did not want to be finished; there was so much he had yet to do in life. He had recently been reading George Borrow's *Lavengro* and some words uttered by Jasper Petulengro came into his mind.

'There's night and day, brother, both sweet things; sun, moon and stars, brother, all sweet things; there's likewise a wind on the heath. Life is very sweet, brother; who would wish to die?'

Yes, life was very sweet; especially when you were no more than twenty-five years old. He did not wish to die.

But there was a numbness in his body now that seemed to be climbing up through his legs and his torso like a creeping death. Would he ever again feel the wind on the heath?

It seemed to be a long time since the *Northern Light* had passed out of his sight. He thought of crying out for help, but who would have heard him? He thought of those words Angela had spoken at parting: 'Take care of yourself, my darling.' And this was how he had taken care of himself. But how could he have acted any differently? If the bullet had your name on it, that was you done for, kaput, worm's meat.

He felt that his whole body was turning to ice. He was no longer aware of the pain in his arm; the arm might not have been there for any awareness that he had of it. But that was true of the entire body; it just did not exist any more; he was nothing but a head floating around without plan or purpose.

The book had gone of course; that unfinished manuscript which he had carried around with him from ship to ship. It was lost for ever. And maybe it had been no good anyway; but he would never know now, because he would never write it again even if he had the chance to do so, which now seemed most unlikely.

He was beginning to lose consciousness and he was making no effort of will to stay awake. Where was the sense in it? It would be no more than a prolongation of the agony. Why not let go now, just let go? Perhaps there was an after-life, perhaps a better land far far away, perhaps –

He let go. No more wind on the heath. No more sweet life. Nothing.

*

The first thing he became conscious of was a voice saying: 'He's coming round.'

Then gradually he realised that he was lying on a bunk, well wrapped-up in blankets; and he knew he was in a ship because of the motion and the throbbing of the engines. What he could not understand was how he came to be there, for the last thing he remembered was floating in the water with the numbness taking over his body and all life gone.

A man was bending over him. 'How are you feeling now?'

He stared up at the man. 'Who are you?' The crazy thought came into his mind that he really was dead and that Charon's boat had been brought up to date as a ship and Charon himself had been transformed to a much younger man in a white jacket.

The man himself put paid to this idea. 'Name's Watkins, but that's immaterial. Important thing is, you're alive. You were damn near a goner, and that's a fact.'

He learned more about it later. It was the little red bulb on his life-jacket that saved him. The rescue ship, devotedly searching in the area where the *Northern Light* had gone down, had found him when all hope of there being any other survivors had almost gone. A lookout had spotted the light as it appeared intermittently when he floated on the crest of a wave, vanishing when he slid into the following trough. The ship had already picked up a few others in a lifeboat, the only one to be successfully launched as the freighter went down; but none of these men were gunners.

'You're a lucky man,' Watkins said.

'Yes,' he said, 'I suppose I am.'

*

He was sent to a hospital in Southport. A doctor on board the rescue ship had done his best on the broken arm, but it needed more attention. When he became convalescent he was allowed to go for walks and sit on a bench in the spring sunshine. His arm was still in a sling and he was dressed in one of those shapeless blue suits which seemed to have been made from flannelette by little old ladies with hand-operated sewing-machines in country cottages.

When he was passed fit again for duty he was allowed to go home on leave. He spent the time pottering around on the farm and visiting old friends. He paid a call one morning at the offices of the *Bury and North Suffolk Morning Post*. Rita was still working there at the reception desk, but she was no longer Miss Webb; she was Mrs Atkins. She was delighted to see him and thought that he was looking well, but thinner. She told him that soon after they were married Cyril had joined the R.A.F. He was now an air-gunner, flying in Lancasters.

'I'm horribly worried about him,' she said. 'It's so dangerous, isn't it? I mean so many of them get shot down.'

'Oh,' Sterne said reassuringly, 'I'm sure he'll be lucky.'

It was a lie of course; he was sure of nothing of the sort. There was no more reason why Cyril Atkins should not be shot down on one of his flights over Germany than there was why he himself should not be lost at sea. They were both in the hands of the gods.

Mr Martin spared him a few moments of his valuable time and assured him that he was not forgotten on *The Post*.

'Boys like you are doing a wonderful job for King and Country. And don't imagine that those of us who, for reasons of age or other considerations, are unable to step into uniform are not conscious of the great debt we owe to you fighting men. We are; yes, most certainly we are. Our thoughts go with you wherever you may be.'

All of which sounded to Sterne too much like the opening sentences of an editorial for the paper. There was a certain lack of sincerity about the words. He doubted whether Arthur Martin had given a single thought to his former employee in the past few years.

'Not,' Mr Martin said, 'that we don't suffer hardships ourselves. For us who keep the home fires burning, so to speak, life is not all cakes and ale. No, not by any means.'

'I'm sure it's not,' Sterne said.

*

He did not see his one-time tennis partner, Phyllis Chambers, but he heard that she was now in the A.T.S. and had a commission. It amused him to reflect that if they ever met when in uniform he would have to salute her and address her as ma'am.

*

One day he went for a cycle ride and found himself in Breckland. At the side of the road was heathland with masses of young green bracken and a few Scots pines growing here and there. There were scarcely any clouds in the sky, and high overhead some almost invisible aircraft were marking the blue dome with long white vapour trails. A light breeze stirred the bracken. It was the wind on the heath and life was very sweet, as Mr Petulengro had said. But tomorrow his leave would be finished and soon he would be at sea again. The War would not stop for him.

Chapter Twenty-One – SOMETHING

It was the meat run to Argentina again this time. A different gun-team, a different ship. The *Ocean Star* was a passenger-cargo liner, fast enough to sail unescorted. The voyage to Buenos Aires via Jamaica was uneventful, the return via Freetown equally so. More beef for the dinner-tables of Britain.

A few weeks later he was in a filthy old steamship on the Russia run to Murmansk in mid-winter. Snow and ice and bitter winds, and attacks from enemy planes and U-boats. No picnic, that. Then more Atlantic convoys, but never the good fortune of another visit to New York. Boston, Philadelphia, and Halifax in Nova Scotia, but never the city he desired so much to see again for one reason only: she was there.

He had heard from her a few times, though she was not much of a letter-writer. The letters sometimes took quite a while to catch up with him. He learned that *Let's Go* was still running and that she was still doing her stint at the Stage Door Canteen. He was not so pleased about that; he thought of all the American servicemen who went there and maybe tried to date her. He felt jealous and frustrated because he could not be with her. He wrote long letters to her and posted them in various ports. He could not be certain that all of them reached her, but he knew that he must have written at least a hundred words for every one of hers that he received in return.

And then, after a long gap with no letter at all, he had one from a different part of America, from a state on the other side of the continent – California. She was in Hollywood.

'Darling David,' she wrote. 'It's all happening to me and I'm being rushed off my feet, so you'll have to excuse this hasty note. I simply haven't the time to write a long letter, but I had to tell you the news. Well, *Let's Go* was finally taken off on Broadway, and what do you think? Just when I was afraid I might be out of a job for goodness knows how long, this sweet man turned up with a truly stupendous offer to go into films. I hardly needed to think about it for a minute before accepting. I mean it's not the sort of chance anyone in their right senses would turn down, and I'm not that stupid. So here I am in Hollywood amongst the stars and things are really moving. No time for more now, but I'll try to keep you posted. All my love, Angela.'

There was a postscript: 'I do hope and pray you haven't been on any more of those dreadful ships that get sunk. You must stay alive. You must, you must. For my sake.'

It was some months since this letter had been written, and he wondered whether she had started filming yet. Although he was always pleased to hear from her and the very handwriting gave him a lift because it was something of hers that he could see and touch, nevertheless the final effect of the letter was depressing. He felt that she was drifting further and further away from him, and not just in the physical sense, though California was on the west coast where he was unlikely ever to set foot. She was obviously still on the way up and would soon be far beyond his reach.

There was another thing in the letter that made him uneasy: it was the word 'sweet' which she had used to describe the man who had so fortunately turned up at the moment when she was out of a job. 'This sweet man' she had called him. Of course it might mean nothing; it might have been a word she had used simply because the fellow had stepped in with this 'truly stupendous' offer, and he had to believe that that was all there was to it; for his peace of mind he had to. But it bothered him all the same.

*

The War was moving against the Axis now. The Russians were advancing on all fronts, having first held and then defeated the German besiegers at Stalingrad; Sicily had been taken by the Allies and Mussolini had been overthrown; Japanese sea power had been crushed by the American Pacific Fleet, and the 14th Army under General Slim was driving the invaders southward down the Malay Peninsula. The tide had really turned at last, but there was still much to be done.

On June the Sixth 1944 Sterne was on board a little coaster which had carried a cargo of ammunition across the Channel to the invasion beaches on the Normandy coast. He had been promoted to the rank of lance-sergeant some time before and was in charge of four gunners and two naval ratings manning four Oerlikon guns. The ship was there for a week discharging its cargo and was to make half a dozen more trips to Mulberry Harbour from the London docks while flying bombs were dropping all over the capital. But he led a charmed life.

One evening he went to the Windmill theatre, which boasted that it had never closed. A man in uniform could get in for five shillings, but only in the gallery. It seemed much the same in many ways as it had been years before. The big difference was that there was no Angela Street on the stage, and without her the show had lost its charm for him.

*

His last voyage was in a tanker, the M.V. *San Antonio*, on the Russia run. The tanker was carrying a cargo of raw alcohol picked up in Philadelphia, and it struck him as curious that after all these years of seagoing he should have been spared until these last few months of the conflict the necessity of sailing in one of the vessels that the old gunlayer named Gregg on board the S.S. *Dagon* had described as hell-ships.

But the Russia run was less hazardous now. The convoy reached the Barents Sea without seeing the least sign of a German plane. Sterne was sharing a cabin with a bearded D.E.M.S. petty officer named Dougal, a Scot from Inverness who could not have been more different from the three of his countrymen who had sailed with him in the ill-fated *Dagon*. Dougal was a large soft-spoken man who had been employed in a dye-works before the War, and the two of them got on very well together.

Dougal was of the opinion that there would be no trouble on this voyage. 'They must know they're finished. They've got nothing to gain by trying to sink our ships now. They can't win now.'

Sterne had to agree that there seemed to be logic in this, but as things turned out it did not prevent a pack of U-boats ganging up on them in the Kola Inlet and sinking two merchant ships and one of the escort vessels. There were snow squalls hitting them at the time, making visibility poor, and it was not pleasant. Everybody was nervous, and with good reason.

Sterne encountered Dougal on the catwalk. 'So much for your assessment of the situation, Jock. Maybe the bastards in the tin cans haven't heard they've lost.'

He was very conscious of the fact that just below the catwalk were many thousands of gallons of alcohol which might behave in a highly volatile and undesirable manner if a torpedo went into it. But there were to be no more sinkings and the rest of the ships reached their destination safely. He felt a great sense of relief. There were no continual air-raids on Murmansk as there had been on his previous visit to that icy port. You could sleep undisturbed at night now.

One day he went ashore with Dougal and watched an American film in a large building which looked as if it might have served as a concert hall. The film was called *Edison the Man*, and Spencer Tracy was playing

Edison. It seemed an odd choice for the Russians to have made. After all, did they not claim to have invented the telephone, the gramophone, the electric light bulb and all the rest of the things that were being credited to the American on the screen? But perhaps the subtitles were correcting the misleading information that the film was giving. Neither Sterne nor Dougal was able to read Russian and therefore could not tell.

*

It was well on into April when they began the homeward voyage and the War was rapidly drawing to a close.

'It would be the devil if we bought it now,' Dougal said. 'Right at the end.'

It was a fear they all had; that the luck would run out at this late stage when they were so close to home. Yet in any war there was always someone who was the last to die. You just hoped it would not be you.

And in the event their luck held. On the very day that World War Two officially ended in Europe the *San Antonio* crept into Loch Long and sent the gulls wheeling away in fright as her anchor chain rattled from the locker in a cloud of rust. They were home and dry.

*

Yet the war with Japan was not yet finished, and would not be until two bombs of unimaginable destructive power had been dropped on Hiroshima and Nagasaki. And whether that had been strictly necessary or whether it had been essentially a political ploy would be a subject of argument for many years to come.

*

David Sterne came to the end of his army career in November 1945, just a few weeks before his twenty-ninth birthday. He felt that he had lost six years of his life – the best years. And what had he done in all that time that was of any real value? Looked at in a cold dispassionate way, the answer had to be: not much. Not bloody much at all, if you wanted the truth. Without his contribution victory would have come at precisely the same time, no sooner and no later. He had not even been an essential cog in the great machine; a drop of oil maybe, which could easily have been dispensed with, since there were so many other drops of equal worth. But that was true of millions of men and women in the forces. Only the top brass, the generals and admirals and air-marshals made much of an individual impression on the overall course of the conflict – and even they were as likely to make the wrong decisions as the right ones. Only in their memoirs, written years after the events, were they infallible in their judgements, brilliant in their strategy and incapable of being influenced by anything so mean as a desire for personal aggrandisement.

Sterne could make none of these claims for himself, except the last. He knew that the part he had played had been small. He knew that many times he had been afraid, that too often he had taken the easy way rather than the more difficult but better one, and that he had never done anything which might have by any chance put him in line for a medal, apart from the campaign stars and suchlike which you got just for being there.

But at least he could say that no misguided decision on his part had ever sent a hundred or a thousand or ten thousand of his own countrymen to their untimely deaths. Again, it was not much perhaps; but it was something.

Chapter Twenty-Two – OCTOPUS

After his discharge he went back to the farm. There was nowhere else for him to go for the present. His brother Will was married and had a farm cottage. George was still living at home and carrying on a rather lukewarm courtship with the daughter of a neighbouring farmer. It was accepted that when his father eventually decided to retire he would have the farmhouse, while the old people would maybe have a small bungalow built for them somewhere nearby. But so far Mr Sterne was still hale and hearty and showed no inclination to relinquish the reins.

David Sterne had no plans. He knew that he would have to decide sooner or later what to do, because the money he had would soon run out and he had no wish to beg from his father. He might perhaps go up to London again, find somewhere to live and resume the writing of short stories. But he knew that even if he could scrape a living for himself at that game – which was doubtful – he could never hope to earn enough to give him any realistic chance of making himself acceptable to a girl who was already on the ladder to success in the world of films.

Not that he knew just what level she had reached on that ladder. He had not heard from her for quite some time, and so had no news of her progress. If she had already appeared in any films, the information had not reached him; but surely she would have let him know. He still wrote to her, but only very occasionally; there seemed to be no point in writing if no reply was forthcoming. He was worried about her; he wondered whether the move to Hollywood had turned out badly. It could so easily have done; the 'sweet man' might have been a rogue, the 'stupendous offer' worthless, a confidence trick. He just did not know.

He had been no more than a couple of weeks at the farm when he had a letter from London which was to give another twist to his career. It was from a man named Osbert Wilkinson.

Wilkinson and he had met when they were both more or less killing time at a camp near Bristol waiting to be demobbed. Though they had been in the same regiment of the Maritime Royal Artillery they had never previously encountered each other. Wilkinson, a gangling studious-looking man with glasses, had been in publishing before the War in a rather minor position, as he himself confessed. He discovered that Sterne was a writer, and this gave them a common interest.

Sterne thought Wilkinson was a bit crazy, but they got on well together and found plenty to talk about. One of these subjects was an idea Wilkinson had of starting up a magazine. He had no desire to go back to his old job; he had had enough of taking orders from other people far less intelligent than himself and wanted to make use of his talents in his own way. At least, that was what he said.

Sterne thought it was not a bad idea, but he could see snags.

'Won't it take a lot of capital?'

'Not as much as you might think.'

'But it's bound to take quite a packet. Have you got any?'

'Frankly, no.'

'So this is all a daydream?'

'Not necessarily. I may be able to find a backer.'

He refused to enlarge on this, but went on to describe the kind of publication he had in mind. He had been impressed by *Lilliput*, a pocket-sized magazine published by the Hulton Press and in fact subsidised by the highly successful *Picture Post*. *Lilliput* was breaking new ground with a mixture of witty short stories, satirical articles, cartoons, amusingly juxtaposed photographs and the occasional artistic nude.

Wilkinson thought he could do something along similar lines, but with improvements. He had a fund of ideas and immense enthusiasm.

'There's a tremendous market out there. People are reading more than ever; they've picked up the habit during the War. Remember all those men on board ship reading anything they could get their hands on – books, magazines, the lot? Men you'd never think of as readers. Well, they aren't going to give it all up when they get back to civvy street, are they?'

'They might,' Sterne said.

'Oh, I don't believe it. It'll go on. We'll become a literate nation at last.'

Sterne laughed. 'And everybody will be buying your magazine?'

'Of course.'

'What are you going to call it? Have you thought of a title?'

'Lots of them. What do you think of *The Scavenger*?'

'Not much. Sounds like a dustmen's trade journal.'

'Maybe you're right. But I'll think of something that will really grab people.'

'How about *Octopus*?'

'You may have something there,' Wilkinson said. 'You may have just the thing.'

*

Sterne had pretty well forgotten about all this when the letter came. He had never regarded the idea as anything more than a castle in the air, with no real substance to it. The letter proved him wrong.

It was written in Wilkinson's large flowing hand and read:

'Dear David, Drop everything and come up to London at once. *Octopus* is being born and I want you to join the team. All details when you arrive. Don't hesitate; this is your big chance and I will not take no for an answer. I shall be expecting you at the above address as soon as possible, or even sooner. Osbert.'

So it was happening, and he had decided to use that title that he, Sterne, had come up with. He was surprised that Wilkinson had got things moving so quickly; but he was an older man and had been in an earlier group for demobbing. Even so, he had certainly lost no time in setting the wheels turning. And where had the money come from?

He was to learn in due course that it had come from an uncle in Birmingham who had a factory turning out gardening tools and similar implements. During the War it had done contract work for the government, and the profits had been considerable. Wilkinson had unashamedly played on his uncle's conscience.

'I hinted that a nephew who had risked his life for his country deserved a bit of help from the moneybags of the family who had stayed at home and done rather well out of the War. He saw that I had a point and coughed up.'

It came as some surprise when Sterne announced that he would be leaving the farm immediately and setting himself up again in London. His mother seemed particularly disappointed.

'So soon? Why, you've only been here a few days.'

'I'm sorry, Mother, but I've been offered an opportunity and it would be foolish not to grab it.'

'What kind of opportunity?' his father asked.

'Working on a magazine.'

'How much are they offering you?'

'The figure has not yet been fixed.' He decided that it might be wisest not to tell them that the magazine had not yet been launched.

His father looked doubtful. 'Well, I hope you know what you're doing.'

He did know what he was doing, but whether it was the right thing was quite another matter. Time alone would tell.

*

The editorial office was in a patched-up building adjoining a bombsite down Hammersmith way where there remained heaps of brick rubble and charred timber. The side of the building was shored up with heavy beams, and Wilkinson said that it was planned eventually to pull it down and rebuild.

'But that may not be for years yet, so we needn't be in any hurry to move. And the rent's reasonable. All in all, it should suit us fine while we're finding our feet.'

There were a couple of single-bedroom flats in the upper part of the building, one of which Wilkinson was occupying. The other he said Sterne could have if he wished.

Sterne thought it was a good idea. It saved him the bother of finding other accommodation; which might not have been easy.

*

Right from the start it seemed to him a pretty crazy venture, even though Wilkinson had managed to gather quite a bit of talent around him. They would meet in a ground-floor room which had been equipped with the paraphernalia of an office: filing cabinets, typewriters, desks, the lot; all secondhand. A telephone had also been installed and there was a fair-sized oak table round which they would sit, drinking endless cups of coffee, smoking cigarette after cigarette, scribbling notes and talking, talking, talking. There really was a lot of talk, not all of it much to the purpose.

There were four others besides Wilkinson and Sterne. Joe Wade was an artist with a talent for the grotesque and bore rather more than a fleeting resemblance to some of his own creations: a wild mop of hair, sharply pointed nose and limbs that seemed to have grown too long for his body, as though they had been stretched on a rack. Norman Lait was a photographer; a small compact man who had travelled much with the British army, shooting with his camera and being shot at with guns for his pains. He had been wounded in the right leg and walked with a limp. Philip Townsend was a cartoonist who specialised in the comic strip.

The last member of the team, but certainly not the least important, was a woman. Her name was Celia Dart, and she was apparently related in some way to Wilkinson. She was thirty-five, red-haired, freckled, plain and lean. She was also as sharp as a pin, had an excellent business brain and a talent for organisation. Without her everything would have slipped into a state of chaos. She kept things on the rails, and her acid tongue could bring others to order in a moment. All the men respected her judgement, and indeed were rather in awe of her.

It was she who found a printer for the magazine and struck a hard bargain. Wilkinson had arranged for his former employers to see to the distribution side of the business. They were publishers mainly of gardening and homecare journals, but agreed to handle *Octopus* at a very reasonable charge. It was planned to give the magazine one hundred and twenty pages measuring approximately eight inches by five and a half, and the cover price was to be one shilling. It was hoped that some advertisers would be attracted to its pages, but that would depend upon sales figures.

They started with high hopes for the magazine's success; but looking back in years to come Sterne could see that it was doomed from the outset. *Lilliput* never succeeded in making a profit and eventually passed away, mourned by many. And *Octopus*, it had to be admitted, never came up to that standard. It staggered on for several months with ever-decreasing sales in a failing market and then sank without trace, the rich uncle in Birmingham having decided that enough was enough and that he could not allow his conscience to lighten his purse any further.

Still, it had been fun while it lasted.

Chapter Twenty-Three – SIMPSON OF THE YARD

He was still submitting stories to other magazines and having some of them accepted. But the fees were small, and without the salary that Wilkinson was paying him he would not have been making a living, though he still had a few hundred pounds put away.

One day Wilkinson said: 'Have you ever thought of using an agent to handle your work?'

The question took Sterne back in his mind to the early days when he had been bitten by a shark in those waters. He told Wilkinson this and of his decision not to be had again.

'I'm not talking about that sort of agent,' Wilkinson said. 'If you're interested I could introduce you to a genuine one. She's a friend of mine and her name is Frederica Lathwell. You could show her some of your stories and she would give an honest opinion. She wouldn't charge you anything for that.'

Sterne thought about it. Then: 'All right. What have I got to lose?'

'Nothing,' Wilkinson said. 'Nothing at all.'

*

Miss Lathwell had an office in Norfolk Street just off The Strand. It did not impress Sterne very favourably when he and Wilkinson visited it by appointment. It was small and cluttered and had a curiously fusty odour, which probably came from the piles of manuscripts lying around. Or it could have been the walls, the paper being blotchy and possibly mildewed. There was a grimy window which might have been said to be keeping out the daylight rather than admitting it, and a small electric fire was providing the heating.

The agent herself was a not unattractive woman in a rather full-blown sort of way. She was dark-haired; the hair being drawn back with a parting in the middle, and her face was somewhat wide, with highish cheekbones that gave her a vaguely oriental look. Her lips were full, giving an impression of sensuality, and she had gold rings dangling from her ears. She was wearing a shapeless woollen jumper with a black skirt and black stockings. She was smoking a Turkish cigarette, and the nicotine stains on her fingers indicated that she smoked a lot. She was probably approaching thirty years of age.

When Wilkinson had made the introduction she took a hard look at Sterne, as if she could estimate a man's literary ability by his physical appearance.

'So,' she said, 'you are David Sterne.'

Sterne agreed that he was. Wilkinson had said so and he was not prepared to contradict a friend.

'And you have some short stories you would like me to handle?'

'If you think they're good enough.'

Wilkinson had told him that Miss Lathwell had taken over the agency fairly recently, after war service in the W.R.N.S. It had been founded in 1930 by an uncle of hers as the Norfolk Literary Agency, and that was the name under which she operated now that the uncle had retired.

'I believe he still has a stake in the business, but she's the boss now and she's very competent, so I'm told. Drives a hard bargain in her clients' interests.'

Miss Lathwell took the three stories that Sterne had brought, glanced at them and put them aside.

'How's that magazine of yours coming along, Osbert?'

'Not so badly.'

'You'll never make a go of it, you know.'

'Don't be so pessimistic, Freddie.'

'I'm not being pessimistic; I'm being realistic. Give you ten to one it doesn't last a year.'

'I never bet.'

'Just as well. You'd lose your money.'

*

'She's wrong about *Octopus*,' Wilkinson said, when they were on their way back from the agency. 'It's a good magazine. It'll pull through.'

But Sterne was beginning to have doubts, and he suspected that Wilkinson was too; though he would not admit it. Maybe *Octopus* was good. But was it good enough? Were any of them? Suppose that kind of magazine and the short story magazines, even those of long standing, were all on the way out. How many of them would still be alive in ten or twenty years' time?

*

It was next day when the telephone in the office rang. Wilkinson answered it, and had a brief exchange of words with the caller at the other end of the line. Then he hung up.

'That was Freddie,' he said. 'She wants you to go round there and have a talk.'

Sterne wondered whether that was a good sign or a bad, but there was only one way to find out. The previous day he had gone to the Norfolk Literary Agency in company with Osbert Wilkinson. This time he went alone and found Miss Lathwell waiting for him. She did not beat about the bush.

'I won't handle them,' she said.

He felt immediately deflated. This was a pretty direct rebuff, and it was not what he had been expecting.

'So you don't think they're good enough?'

'It's not that,' she said. 'In fact they're very well written and they could quite possibly find a market. But you don't need an agent to sell them for you; you can do it just as well yourself and save the commission; which, to be entirely frank with you, wouldn't really be worth my while bothering with.'

'I see.'

She must have sensed his disappointment; she would have had to be very insensitive indeed not to have done so, and she gave a sudden smile which altogether transformed her face and made it really quite charming, he thought.

'Now don't be downhearted,' she said. 'I haven't brought you here just to give you a kick in the teeth. In fact, from what I have seen of your work, I'm quite convinced that you have it in you to make the grade. But not perhaps with short stories. That's an awfully difficult field to plough; and the market is shrinking in spite of all those little magazines like *New Writing* and *Modern Reading* and *Seven* and *Writing Today* – and, of course, *Octopus*. They won't survive for very much longer, and I doubt whether even the old ones like *Strand* and *Argosy* will either.'

'This is a gloomy picture you're painting.'

'It is. And I may be wrong, but I think it's a true one. There are the women's magazines of course. They take short stories, but not the sort that you write. So here's what I'm going to suggest, and it's up to you to make the decision. Why don't you write a novel? Have you ever thought about it?'

'Oh yes. I started one once. Maybe got about two thirds of it written.'

'So what happened to it?'

'It went to the bottom of the Atlantic with the ship I was sailing in.'

'Ah yes. Osbert told me you were in that business. It's a kind of link, isn't it? Between you and me. I was in the Wrens, but it was a shore job, of course.'

He thought it was rather a tenuous link; but if she liked to make it, why not?

'Anyway,' she said, 'I think you should try again. And here's another suggestion: why not write a whodunit?'

'A detective novel?'

'Yes. There's always a market for them. And the advantage is that once you've got your main character up and running you can go on using him over and over again. If readers get to know and like him you've got a captive audience, as it were. They'll come back for more of the same.'

'But I don't know anything about crime writing.'

She brushed this objection aside. 'Oh, you'll soon pick it up. The pattern is more or less standard. You have a victim or victims; you get together a lot of suspects with strong motives for committing the crime; you leave a shoal of red herrings lying around; and gradually your sleuth works his way to the real murderer, who is of course the most unlikely one of the lot.'

'You make it sound very simple.'

'Basically, it is. It's up to the individual writer to introduce variations on the theme. So what do you say? Are you willing to have a go?'

'I'll think about it,' Sterne said.

*

'Well?' Wilkinson said. 'How did it go?'

'She refused to handle the stories.'

'Oh dear. Didn't she like them?'

'Actually, I believe she did, rather. But she said I could do as well with them as she could – and save the percentage. Then she suggested I should write a crime novel.'

'Are you going to?'

'I said I'd think about it.'

*

He thought about it for a couple of days and decided to have a shot at it. That was when Detective Inspector Hector Simpson was born – Simpson of the Yard. He wrote the book, *A Web of Deceit*, in two months in his spare time from working on the magazine.

He gave it to Osbert Wilkinson to read. He liked it.

'David, old man, I think you've found your métier.'

'I just hope Miss Lathwell thinks the same.'

*

Frederica Lathwell was not quite so enthusiastic. She suggested some revision to improve the story. Sterne hated re-writing, but he took her advice and did the revision. Finally she gave her approval of the finished work and agreed to handle it.

'So what happens now?'

'As far as you're concerned,' she said, 'nothing at all. Perhaps for many moons. Publishers are notoriously dilatory. But please, David, promise me one thing.'

'What's that?'

'That you won't keep ringing me up to ask how things are going. I'll let you know at once if there's any news.'

He promised not to be a pest and went away to wait in silence while Simpson of the Yard was sent off on his travels.

Chapter Twenty-Four – VICTIM

The letter came in a cheap buff envelope. It had been forwarded to him by a magazine which had published one of his stories. She must have seen his name above the story and decided to take that way of getting in touch with him. The notepaper had the same shoddy look as the envelope; it was ruled and might have been torn out of an exercise-book. The handwriting ignored the lines and went scrawling across the page like the track of a spider that had dipped its feet in an inkpot. He had seen that writing before. It had been a long time ago, but he recognised it at once.

'Dear David,' he read, 'I know I have no right to ask this of you, but I beg for old time's sake that you will come and see me. There are things I so much wish to put straight. Do please come. Petra Lakos.'

There was an address. It was in Canning Town.

He wondered what she meant by putting things straight. What was there to put straight? He had not thought of her or Peter for a very long time. He had imagined they were still in prison, but it appeared that she at least had been set free. He was glad that it was so – for her sake. He would of course go to see her; no question about that.

*

He travelled out by Tube, getting off at the West Ham station. After a good deal of walking and several inquiries he found the place. It was a bed-sitter up one flight of carpetless stairs. The house smelled of boiled cabbage and dry rot. There was a number on the door and he rapped on it with his knuckles. He heard her voice, quavering a little.

'Who is it?'

'David Sterne.'

There was a sound of bolts being slid back, and then the door opened and she was standing there.

'Come in,' she said. 'Do come in.'

He was shocked by her appearance. Her hair was dead white and she had thinned down to a mere shadow of her former self. She looked old, really old, the skin of her face one mass of wrinkles, as though when the flesh had melted away it had collapsed in upon itself. She was wearing some old clothes that she must have had before her arrest. They were much too big for her now and hung loosely on her much diminished frame.

He went in and she closed the door and locked it. She motioned him to a chair.

'Please sit down.'

It was an armchair, rather threadbare. The entire room looked pretty wretched; he supposed she rented it furnished and could afford nothing better. The bed was concealed by a curtain.

'You will drink a cup of tea?' she asked.

'Oh,' he said, 'don't bother.'

'It will be no bother, I assure you; no bother at all.'

He did not persist in his refusal because he knew that it would give her pain. He remembered their first meeting when she had given him tea and cake. So long ago; a lifetime, it seemed. This time there was no cake but a dry biscuit to go with the tea that she made in a little niche which served as a kitchen.

She sat down facing him. She stared at him for a while in silence, as though refreshing her memory of him.

'You have not altered greatly,' she said, 'though of course you are older. You have seen fighting, perhaps?'

'I was in the army,' he said. But he did not go into details.

'Yes, of course. But now you are out and writing again.'

'Yes.'

His gaze moved round the room, and she noticed it.

She said: 'You are wondering where Peter is.'

It had in fact been in his mind. He supposed Lakos must still be in prison.

'He is dead,' she said. 'Three years ago. We were never allowed to see each other, you know.'

Sterne did not know what to say. He mumbled: 'I'm sorry.'

'Oh, it is so long ago, so long ago. Time heals, they say. It isn't true. It doesn't. Not entirely.'

Still she had said nothing regarding the purpose of the visit, the putting of things straight. He thought it time to give a hint.

'You were going to tell me something.'

'Of course. I have not forgotten. But it is painful, so very painful. You believe no doubt that Peter was an evil man; that I too was evil.'

'No, no.'

'But how could you think otherwise? We had been working for the Nazis. We had betrayed the country that had given us a refuge. We had even misled you into believing we were just harmless eccentrics. Is it not so?'

'Well –'

'Of course it is. But there was a reason. Peter had a brother in Germany. Otto was married with two children. The Gestapo got hold of them and discovered the connection. They threatened all kinds of atrocities against that poor family if Peter did not co-operate. A letter came from Otto begging him to do as the Gestapo demanded; if not for his sake, for the sake of his wife and children. What else could Peter do? You see the terrible position he was in. He detested the very idea of helping the Nazis, but the alternative was to condemn his brother and his brother's family to unimaginable horrors. Now do you understand?'

'Yes,' Sterne said, 'I understand.'

'And in the end what was the use of it?' She spoke bitterly. 'They all died just the same in a concentration camp. The betrayal had been for nothing.'

Before leaving Sterne took out his wallet. 'I would like to help if –'

But she refused to accept anything. 'I am not in want. I need very little. I simply wished for you to know the truth. And now perhaps you will not think so badly of me and Peter.'

He assured her that he would not, and she gave a wan little smile.

'We always loved you, you know. You were like a son to us.'

*

It was two days later when the police contacted him to tell him that Petra Lakos was dead. She had written his name and address on a card, and then she had taken the overdose that had killed her. They knew of no one else who had any connection with her, so they came to him.

He had to give evidence at the inquest, and a verdict of accidental death was returned, since there was nothing to prove that she had intended to kill herself. But he himself was certain that she had. What had she left to live for?

He made the funeral arrangements. On the day of the burial it rained heavily. Wilkinson went along with him to keep him company. They were the only mourners. It was a miserable affair. Poor Petra; just one more victim of that vicious megalomaniac who had taken his own life in the Berlin bunker.

Chapter Twenty-Five – **END OF THE ROAD**

It was in an evening paper that he had picked up from a news-vendor. The headline ran: 'STARLET WEDS STAR'. There was a not very good photograph of the happy couple and a brief account of the Hollywood wedding of 'Up-and-coming young British actress, Angela Street, to long-time filmstar, Leopold Lester'. Lester had been married three times before, but for Miss Street it was her first venture into matrimony. The two had been playing opposite each other in a film and had fallen in love for real on the set.

There was more, but he would not read it. He crumpled the paper into a ball and shoved it into a litter bin. He was shattered. He found it quite incredible that she should have fallen for a man like that, a fifty-year-old ham actor with three wives and a string of love affairs behind him. She must have been out of her mind. And all this had happened without a word from her to him. He had been left to find out about it from a newspaper. Had she no more consideration for him than that?

This of course explained the lack of letters from her of recent months. She could not be bothered to write to him because she had been too much involved with this damned film and the bastard who was acting with her.

He had had a premonition of something of this sort when she left New York and dashed off to California. In the make-believe hothouse of Hollywood people lost all grip on reality; they went completely off the rails. But this –

*

He told Wilkinson; he had to confide in someone; he could not keep it all bottled up. Naturally enough, Wilkinson was less shattered by the news than he had been.

'Don't take it so hard. It's not the end of the world, you know. Plenty more pebbles on the beach.'

Which might well have been true, but none of them was the one pebble that he desired.

'She'll regret it,' he said. 'She's bound to. It'll never work.' This was what he hoped. He could not bring himself to wish her well in her marriage; that would have been asking too much. 'I'm the one who really got her started, you know.'

'You?'

'Yes. I wrote a feature about her for a magazine. It gave her the publicity she needed.'

He knew this was pretty far from the truth even as he was saying it. All that the feature had done was to lose her her job at the Windmill and put into print that fantasy about the vicar in Yorkshire and the travelling concert party called The Streamers. But he was not going to tell Wilkinson that.

*

He heard from her some days later. There was a wedding photograph in the envelope and nothing else. No letter. On the back of the photograph was just one word: 'Sorry!'

He remembered a time in the past when she was sorry and left him. It had been a quite inadequate word to express his feelings then, and it was now.

Sorry! She was sorry! Christ! What did she think he was? Sorry! Was that all she could say? Had she no time even for a brief note?

Yet what could she have said? Nothing that would have softened the blow; there were no words that could have done that. Ah, but to send this photograph! She should not have done that; it was a knife turning in the wound. She looked radiant in her bridal dress; and beside her stood that ogre, that troll, that abortion. By the world Lester was regarded as a handsome man; to Sterne he was a Quasimodo.

In a fit of rage he tore the photograph into little pieces and flushed them down the lavatory pan. If he could have done the same to the man he would gladly have done so.

*

Acting on a whim, he went down to the East End and paid a call on the Maggses. He supposed they would have heard about their daughter's marriage, but he doubted very much whether they had attended the ceremony. They would hardly have fitted in.

There had been a lot of bomb damage in that part of London; entire streets of houses had been demolished. But though much of the surrounding area had been heavily bombed, the greengrocery shop had miraculously escaped serious damage.

Alfie and Queenie were delighted to see him, though obviously surprised by the visit. They insisted on his staying to eat with them, and it was not until they were halfway through the meal that anyone mentioned the subject that was undoubtedly uppermost in all their minds. Then, as though he could no longer keep it battened down, Alfie burst out:

'Well, she's gorn an' done it now.'

'You're talking about Angela, of course,' Sterne said.

'I'm talking about Maggie. Why is it, I ask you, that she 'as this knack of picking wrong'uns? First there was that bastard, Judas, and now this bleeder.'

'Now, now, Alf,' Mrs Maggs said soothingly. 'We don't know as there's anything wrong with him.'

'Well, it stands to reason, don't it? Married three times afore; old enough to be 'er dad. Does that sound like a bloke you'd want for a son-in-law?'

'Not really, no. It don't seem very nice. I wish it'd been somebody else.'

Mr Maggs looked hard at Sterne. 'Fact is, we 'oped it'd be you. That time arter you was 'ere Ma an' me, we thought she'd come to 'er senses and got the right one at last. But it looks like it wasn't to be, more's the pity.'

Sterne felt embarrassed. It was difficult to know what to say. 'I should have liked –' he said, and stopped, tongue-tied.

'She told us in a letter she'd seen you in New York,' Mrs Maggs said. 'She seemed so pleased. We thought then –'

'So she writes to you?'

'Not often. She's never been the one for that. But she seemed real worried about you – in the convoys and that. Pity you couldn't have stayed there with her.'

Sterne was beginning to wonder whether it had been wise to pay this visit. Their undisguised sympathy for him; their wish that he could have been their son-in-law rather than the aging film actor; all this served rather to open the wound than to heal it. In their presence he could only feel more painfully the loss of the girl he was still so deeply in love with.

He managed to get away soon after the meal. They urged him to come again.

'Any time, any time,' Alfie said. 'You're always welcome 'ere. Though I reckon you're a busy man these days.'

'Pretty busy.'

'Well, don't forget. Always pleased to see you. Ain't we, Ma?'

'Oh yes,' Queenie said. 'Nobody we like better. And you know where to find us.'

*

He thought of ringing the Norfolk Literary Agency to ask Freddie Lathwell whether there was any news of the book; it was more than a month since she had taken it. But then he remembered her admonition to him that he was not to bother her in that way and he curbed the urge. If she had anything to report she would get in touch with him; and she had warned him that he would need to be patient.

Octopus was still alive but not kicking very vigorously. A feeling of depression appeared to have settled on the little group which sat round the table in the office and planned the forthcoming numbers of the magazine. The earlier enthusiasm had gone, and indeed it was difficult to look forward with any optimism to the future when it was all too plain to see that for *Octopus* there really was no future.

Only Wilkinson refused to face the fact; still arguing that all would come right in the end.

'Perhaps if we were to lower the price, sell it at ninepence.'

Celia Dart said bluntly: 'If you brought it down to sixpence it still wouldn't work the trick. The public obviously don't want it at any price.'

'If we were to make some changes in the layout —'

'What changes?'

'I don't know. We could maybe think of something. Anyone got any suggestions?'

Nobody volunteered anything.

Joe Wade said: 'It's pretty good as it is. No amount of tinkering with it is going to make much difference. Maybe we started too late. Maybe the days of this type of magazine are numbered.'

'We couldn't have started any sooner,' Wilkinson said. 'We were all doing another job, remember?'

It was still to be another few months before he was forced to admit defeat. That was when the uncle in Birmingham cut off the life-giving cash supply. Sterne was with him when the letter came. It was brief but to the point.

'The mean old bastard,' Wilkinson said. 'No faith. No gratitude. That's the older generation for you. Well, it looks like the end of the road for *Octopus*.'

'What'll you do now?'

'I suppose I shall have to go back to the gardening and homecare journals. The good earth and the bricks and mortar. Ah well!'

'Will they have you?'

'The buggers had better,' Wilkinson said. 'They'd bloody well better.'

Chapter Twenty-Six – CELEBRATION

By a strange coincidence on the day when *Octopus* finally hit the buffers Sterne had a call from Miss Lathwell. Wilkinson had answered the telephone and had handed it over to him.

'It's Freddie.'

Sterne's heart gave a jump. Because this had to be news of the book, good or bad. Annoyingly, she refused to go into any details on the phone; all she would say was that she had to have a talk with him and would he come round straightaway? It was the middle of the afternoon, and even if he had had all sorts of other things lined up he would have thrust them aside. But there was nothing, and he said he would be on his way at once.

He travelled by Tube and got off at the Temple and walked the rest of the way, and his pulse was working overtime when he mounted the stairs leading up to Miss Lathwell's office. He had a dreadful feeling that she was just going to hand the manuscript back to him and tell him it was no go. For if there had been any good news to impart she would surely have given some hint of it on the phone.

She greeted him remarkably calmly, and he took this as a bad sign and prepared himself for the worst.

'I'm so glad you could come,' she said. 'What's the weather like out there?'

'It's cold but dry,' he said. But what in hell had the weather got to do with anything? Why didn't she get to the point? Why was she keeping him on tenterhooks like this?

And then suddenly she gave that smile which seemed to transform her face and make her quite beautiful.

'No,' she said, 'this is very naughty of me. I should have told you on the phone, but I wanted to see your reaction and I couldn't resist teasing you a little.'

But she was still teasing him, still not getting to the point. And then she gave another smile and said:

'We've won. Reed and West like it. They want to publish. I've got a contract for you to sign.'

It was fortunate that there was a chair near at hand because he had to sit down. He knew that he should have said something, but the words would not come.

'Well,' she said, 'I thought you'd be rather pleased. It is what you wanted to hear, isn't it?'

'Yes, of course. It's just that it hasn't quite sunk in.'

'It will,' she said. 'They're offering an advance of seventy-five pounds, which is not over-generous but is about right for a first book.'

He would have accepted no advance at all. Just to have the book published, that was the thing. Seventy-five pounds seemed a lot to him; it was ten times as much as he was getting for most of the stories which he managed to sell.

'That's against a royalty of ten per cent on the selling price of ten-and-six. It rises to twelve-and-a-half on sales from three thousand to six thousand, and fifteen percent thereafter. Frankly, you're not likely to reach the top figure with this book, so it's academic.'

She handed him the typed contract to read. He glanced through the four pages without taking it all in. There were clauses regarding the paper, the printing, the jacket, foreign rights, paperback rights, film rights, book clubs, cheap editions, remainders, libel . . .

He said: 'I suppose you've checked all this?'

'Naturally.'

'And it's all right?'

'It's very much the standard agreement. They vary a bit from publisher to publisher, but not a lot. You wouldn't be likely to get anything better than this anywhere else. I'd advise you to accept it.'

He had never had the slightest intention of doing anything else. He would have been crazy not to accept. He noticed that the publishers were taking an option on his next two books.

'What does that mean?'

'It means you're bound to give them the first offer of whatever you write next.'

'But they don't have to accept it?'

'No. They've got you, but you haven't got them if they don't like what you send them next time.'

'Isn't that rather one-sided?'

'Well, look at it this way: it's their money that's at risk. It costs a lot to launch a book. All you supply is the genius.'

She was smiling again, indicating that this was her little joke. And then she said: 'Are you doing anything this evening?'

'Nothing in particular. Why?'

'I was thinking, if it appeals to you, we might have a small celebration. My treat.'

'Well, I –'

'You don't have to. Though it is quite an occasion, isn't it? But of course if you'd rather not –'

He felt that he could hardly refuse. It would have been a snub, boorish. And when he came to think about it, the prospect of an evening on the town with Freddie Lathwell certainly had its attractions. It would be no penance.

'No,' he said. 'I'd be very pleased. It sounds a great idea.'

She was pleased too; he could see that. 'So it's settled. Incidentally, R and W would like you to call in tomorrow morning at eleven o'clock to discuss the book. You can manage that?'

'Certainly.'

*

They had dinner in a little Italian restaurant which she seemed to know well, and where she was known by the proprietor. She ordered champagne. Obviously she believed in celebrating in style.

'Tell me,' Sterne said, 'do you celebrate like this with all your clients when you place a book for them?'

'Don't be ridiculous,' she said. 'Of course not.'

'So why me?'

'You're different. You're rather special, aren't you?'

'Am I?'

'Didn't you know?'

He thought the wine must be going to her head, but she seemed quite sober. Happy but not inebriated. Free from the cares of business, she seemed to have loosened up and was enjoying herself. Enjoying the company too, apparently. Well, for that matter he was also enjoying the evening.

He said: 'You were right about *Octopus*, you know. The rich uncle who was backing it pulled out, so we're closing down.'

'I didn't know. That means you'll be out of a job, I suppose?'

'Well, yes. But I shan't be on my uppers just yet. I've got a bit to tide me over.'

'What about the flat? Will you be able to keep it?'

'I don't know. It rather went with the magazine. I may have to look for somewhere else.'

'I'm sorry about the magazine. But it really was a mad idea.'

'I suppose so.'

'Typical of Osbert, of course. He always was potty.'

*

They ended up at her place. Looking back afterwards he could see that it had been her intention from the outset. Her place was also a flat, but of a far different sort from the one he had been living in. It was not particularly large, just the one bedroom, but it was very elegant. It looked the kind of home that would be occupied by a woman of taste and means. Freddie apparently scored on both counts.

They sat on a comfortably upholstered sofa in front of an electric fire and listened to soft music on the radio and drank pink gin and talked. And gradually they moved closer together and started doing things with their hands and talking less and less.

Some time later he found himself sharing a bath with her, and he could see that she had quite a pleasant body even if it was a trifle plump. She had let her hair down now in more senses than one, and there could not have been a sharper contrast between this seductive creature and the tough-bargaining businesswoman of the Norfolk Street office.

From the bath they moved into the bed, and this again had almost certainly been the way she had planned it. Not that he felt like complaining. All in all, it had been quite a day for him: *Octopus* had died, his book had been accepted, and he and Freddie Lathwell had become lovers.

For it was to be no fleeting encounter. He was to leave the other flat and move in with her. He would be there for the next two years.

'I love you, David,' she said. 'I knew it from the first day when Osbert brought you to the office. I knew you had to be mine.'

He did not love her, though he told her he did. He still loved someone else, but she was beyond his reach. So what the hell if he lied! It pleased Freddie and hurt no one.

*

He worked at the flat when she had gone to the office. Then, when there was no one to disturb him, he could really get a lot of writing done. The second Simpson of the Yard novel was finished before the first one came out. It was accepted very quickly.

The first one, *A Web of Deceit*, created no great stir when it appeared, but it was well reviewed and had useful sales figures. Freddie said it was about what she had expected, and the next one, *Dead on Time*, ought to do better. It did. The third, *A Load of old Bones*, was taken in the United States and in all the Scandinavian countries. It was also made into a radio serial. Simpson was becoming quite a well-known character, and Freddie said there was no reason why he should not go on writing about him indefinitely.

'The advantage these literary sleuths have over us ordinary mortals is that they never grow any older; they can remain in the prime of life until the author either dies or becomes too senile to keep them going any longer.'

Sterne was not sure it was a prospect he greatly relished. Would it not become something of a treadmill? Freddie said there was nothing wrong with treadmills if they brought in the cash. He thought this was a pretty mercenary way of looking at things, but he could see that from her point of view it probably was the only way. As an agent her job was to make the maximum amount of money from a client's work, and incidentally, of course, to increase her commission.

*

He had been living with her for about a year when he heard that Angela Street and Leopold Lester had split up. He was not surprised; it was a wonder that the marriage had lasted as long as it had. The film in which the two of them had appeared together had been shown in London and had been panned by the critics, but he had not gone to see it. He knew it would only have enraged him.

He wondered whether the divorce would affect him in any way, and was forced to the conclusion that it would not. She was still in Hollywood, far away from him, and the odds were that she would soon pick up another lover from the crowds of eligible men out there.

Meanwhile his relationship with Freddie moved on into its second year, and he was beginning to feel a certain distaste for the position he was in. He was paying a share of their living expenses, but the fact remained that the flat was hers and he was there more or less as a dependent. He had to admit that she never abused her authority in that respect, but it irked him nevertheless and he felt that it could not be allowed to go on indefinitely. He had to break away.

Still, however, he did nothing about it; he just let things slide. And perhaps the break would have been postponed still further if it had not been for the incident that was to bring matters to a head and relieve him of the necessity of telling her that he wished to end the liaison and depart.

Chapter Twenty-Seven – SPLIT

He went down to the farm for a visit. His mother had been urging him to. 'We hardly ever see you these days,' she wrote in one of her letters. 'Do come and stay for a while.'

So he went. It was to have been for a fortnight, but boredom soon set in, and three days before the time was up he made an excuse for returning to London. He arrived one evening without having given Freddie any warning that he would be coming and let himself into the flat with his key.

The sound of music was audible even before he opened the door; it was coming from the radio in the sitting-room, but there was no one in there who might have been listening to it. He saw that the door of the bedroom was slightly ajar, and he pushed it open and went in.

There were two of them on the bed – Freddie and a man he had never seen before – and they were being very energetic. He could hear the man grunting. A quilt which might initially have covered them had slipped to one side and was trailing on the floor, revealing the fact that Freddie and the man were both stark naked.

She was the first to notice that there was now a third person in the room. She turned her head and saw him in the doorway. Immediately an expression of anger came over her face and she screamed at him:

'Get out of here! Go away, damn you; go away!'

The man now lifted his head and looked at Sterne, and it was plain to see that he was pretty disconcerted at being discovered in that situation. He was a rather portly individual, fortyish, with curly black hair and a bald spot on the crown. He had so much body hair that the idiotic thought flashed in to Sterne's head that he could well have dispensed with underclothing.

'O God!' he said. 'Oh my God!'

His first reaction seemed to be an urge to get himself out of sight, and he rolled over to the side of the bed opposite the door, tumbled over the edge and disappeared from view.

Sterne had not moved, and now Freddie screeched at him again, obviously in a furious temper: 'Get out! Get to hell out of here!'

He retreated then, closing the door behind him. But he did not leave the flat. He was damned if he was going to allow himself to be thrust out into the cold just because Freddie had taken another man to bed with her. Admittedly this was her flat, but it was for the present his home also.

So he switched the radio off and went into the kitchen and made himself a cup of coffee. He left the kitchen door ajar so that he could hear when the hairy man with the pod took his leave – as he felt certain he would do – and when sounds from the sitting-room indicated that this had happened he returned to hear what Freddie had to say for herself.

She was in there. She was in a dressing-gown and was smoking one of her favourite Abdullah cigarettes. In her left hand she was holding a generous glass of pink gin and she was standing by the mantelpiece. She glared at him when he walked in.

'What in hell are you doing back here?' she demanded. 'You weren't due back until the end of the week.'

He answered ironically: 'Would you believe me if I told you I couldn't bear to stay away from you a day longer?'

'No, I bloody well wouldn't,' she said. 'And don't try to be funny because I'm not in the mood for it.'

'No, I can see that. Apparently you were in the mood for something, but I wouldn't call it humour.'

'And you don't have to be so damned sarcastic either. I suppose you don't approve?'

'Does it matter whether I approve or not? I just think you might have mentioned that you'd be having someone else in to fill the gap while I was away. Are you going to tell me who he was?'

'I don't see the necessity. Let's just say he was someone it suited me to invite round. Someone who happened to please me.'

'Well,' Sterne said, 'I could see he was doing that. I didn't know you had such a taste for the beer-belly hairy type. If I'd known I might have bought a hair-shirt for wearing in bed, though I don't know what I could have done about the gut. A cushion maybe.'

This remark seemed to touch some nerve and really throw her into a fury. She spat out some words which he felt sure she must have picked up during her spell in the Navy, like the taste for pink gin. And then she threw the gin in his face.

'You bastard!' she said. 'So this is what it comes to. I set you on your feet. I do everything for you. I give you a roof over your head, a place where you can write, and this is what I get for my pains. Insults. Well, I should have known you were a rat, a bloodsucker, a filthy parasite.'

He thought she was laying it on a bit thick; because whatever she had done for him had been done for her profit as well as his. And apart from the use of the flat, any other reputable agent could probably have done as much. But he knew what was really galling her: it was the fact that he had discovered her in that most undignified of situations in the bedroom. She would never forgive him for that.

One thing was pretty certain: she did not love him any more. But he felt that that had been so for some time, and if they parted company now it was not likely to break the heart of either of them. The time had come for it, and that was that.

As if to emphasise the fact, she said: 'You don't live here any more. As of now you're out.'

'Well,' he said, 'I think, all things considered, that would be for the best.' He was mopping the gin off his face with a handkerchief. 'But I hope you'll allow me to spend one more night here.'

'Not in my bed, you scum.'

'No. In the circumstances that would probably not be advisable.'

*

He spent the night on the sofa and slept remarkably well. He had a feeling of relief at having regained his freedom. Only now did he fully realise how much of a burden the liaison with Freddie had become. The final split might have been made in a less vituperative manner, but the essential point was that it had been made. Now he could go his own way and never need consider whether any action he might take would meet with her approval. Yes, it was good to be free.

In the morning he packed a bag and asked whether she objected to his leaving his typewriter and books and the rest of the gear he had accumulated until he found other accommodation. She answered coldly that it did not bother her, and he could keep the key until he had cleared everything out.

He thought she seemed to be in rather low spirits, and he wondered whether she was regretting her haste in turning him out. Perhaps she would have been prepared to change her mind after all if she could have seen a way of doing so without injury to her pride. But he was careful not to give her any encouragement in this respect; and maybe he was wrong anyway; maybe she was as glad to be shot of him as he was to go. It was probably the manner of the parting that she found depressing, and she might have been feeling somewhat ashamed of her outburst of the previous evening. It had certainly not been very creditable.

*

He took up temporary lodging in a hotel and began looking around for something more permanent. Within a few days he had found a suitable place for rent within easy walking distance of Lord's cricket ground. In the summer he would be able to drop in and watch a match whenever he felt like it. The property, which was described by the agents as a furnished maisonette of superior quality, was quite small, but it would have been far too expensive for him a couple of years ago; now his finances were in much better shape.

When he had removed the last of his gear from Freddie's place he returned the key to her at the office in Norfolk Street. There now arose the question of whether or not she was to continue to act as his agent, and he broached the subject.

'What do you think?' she said. 'Do you want to find someone else to handle your work?'

'Frankly, no. I just thought you might no longer care to act for a rat, a bloodsucker and a filthy parasite.'

She grinned suddenly. 'Oh God!' she said. 'I did rather blow my top that evening, didn't I? I don't often do that, you know.'

'You had provocation,' he said. 'Let's forget it, shall we?'

She was a good agent and he saw no reason at all for leaving her, while she was too shrewd a businesswoman to reject a client who was likely to become increasingly profitable to her as the years went by.

So the business association survived, though the other one had ended. It was the sensible way.

Chapter Twenty-Eight – TRYST

He had been living in the maisonette for a couple of months and had almost completed the fifth of the Simpson of the Yard novels. Spring was giving way to summer and he had already paid a few visits to Lord's. He found that watching cricket was something he could do while still jotting down ideas and bits of narrative for the novel. He took a notebook with him for this purpose, and it seemed to quieten the small voice of conscience which tried to tell him that he ought to be at work rather than sitting in the sun and watching a pack of men in white clothing knocking a leather ball around with wooden bats and chasing it all over the greensward. It was quite a ridiculous pastime if you really thought about it.

It was on a day when he had just returned from one of these pleasant little outings that the telephone started ringing. When he answered a voice said:

'Hi, David! Guess who.'

He knew at once. Even on the phone, even after all this time of not hearing it, he could not mistake that voice. It was the only one that could have set his pulse racing as it did.

'Angela!'

'None other. Surprise, surprise!'

His immediate thought was that she was calling from Hollywood and that the call would be costing the devil of a lot, and how in hell had she got hold of the telephone number? It was amazing too how clearly her voice was coming through across that vast distance; almost as though she were in the same town. And then it struck him that she was in the same town and that she had got his number from Telephone Enquiries, since he was not yet in the book.

'You're in London?'

'Of course. I got in yesterday.'

'Do your people know?'

'Yes. I've been to see them.'

'But why are you here? Are you filming?'

He thought it might be a location job; a London background; that sort of thing. But she killed this idea.

'No, nothing like that. But look, we can't talk about everything over the phone. We've got to meet. Are you busy tomorrow?'

If he had been up to the eyes in work it would have made no difference; he would have put it all aside at a word from her.

'No, not busy at all. Where should we meet?'

'How about the old place? Trafalgar Square.'

So she remembered, as of course he did, and always would. He said it would be fine, and they fixed a time, and he spent the rest of the day thinking about it. He woke up in the night and did some more thinking about it. He could think of nothing else. The hours seemed to pass all too slowly, and his impatience was such that he was on his way to the rendezvous long before it was necessary to do so.

Fortunately it was a fine morning, and he strolled around, scanning the faces of all the girls and young women who were doing the same, in the hope that she might be early too. And in the end it was she who found him. He felt a light touch on his shoulder and turned, and there she was, smiling at him.

'I thought it was you,' she said. 'How awful if I'd made a mistake.'

'You look lovely,' he said. They were the first words that came into his head. He had not seen her since that night in her dressing-room in New York when he had had to leave so soon to join that doomed ship, the *Northern Light*. If he had known then! If she had known! But it would have made no difference; he would still have had to go. 'So long ago,' he said, scarcely realising what he was saying; merely voicing the thought that was in his mind.

But she caught his meaning in an instant. 'Yes, so long ago. Too long.' And then: 'Oh, David! Oh, my darling!' she said. And they were kissing.

The pigeons were waddling around, the stone lions watched impassively, Nelson on top of his column stared straight ahead, the fountains sent their plumes of water into the air, and people came and went. They were oblivious to everything but each other.

'Do you remember,' he said, 'that day when we took shelter in the National Gallery and you told me all those lies about yourself?'

'Yes, of course I remember. It was fun, wasn't it?'

'We don't need to go in there today. Should we just stroll around and talk?'

'That sounds a marvellous idea. There's such a lot to talk about, isn't there? But tell me something first, because it's important. Is there anyone?'

He knew what she was asking and he was glad he and Freddie had split up and he could answer honestly: 'No one. And you?'

'No one.'

'I'm glad.'

'Me too.'

They strolled aimlessly, talking all the time. They found themselves walking down Whitehall and had no idea how they came to be there. Later it was the Victoria Embankment, and later still they were having lunch in a restaurant near Leicester Square. In the afternoon they came, quite by chance it seemed, to the Windmill Theatre.

'This,' he said, 'is where it all started. You gave me the brush-off. Remember?'

She laughed. 'So I did. I thought you were just like all the others.'

'But I wasn't?'

'No,' she said. 'Far from it.'

He had learned by then that she was not in London for any filming purposes. That was all behind her.

'You're not going back to Hollywood?'

'Never. It's a terrible place. Oh, I liked it at first. I suppose I was just dazzled by it all. But it's so unreal. Everybody's playing a part, off the set as well as on it.'

He wondered whether that included Leopold Lester and how much that particular character had contributed to her disenchantment with Tinseltown. But he did not ask. Maybe some day he would hear the story, but not now.

He asked her what she was planning to do, and she said she had decided to go back to the stage. That was where she was really at home, not in films. She missed the rapport you got with a real live audience.

'And have you anything particular in view?'

'I've had feelers. There's a new musical being planned for the West End, and there could be a part for me. It's all pretty much up in the air for the moment, but something may come of it.'

She asked him about the place where he was living now, and said she would like to look at it. So they went back there in the evening and she liked it.

'It's nice.'

'I don't suppose it's much like the luxury you've been used to in Hollywood.'

'Luxury can be so boring,' she said. 'And anyway, this is a lot better than the flat in Rosetta Avenue.'

'So you haven't forgotten that?'

'As if I ever could! Sometimes I think they were the happiest days of my life. We had nothing and it was just heaven.'

'For me as well.'

'Really and truly?'

'Yes, really and truly.'

She noticed his books and the paperbacks and the foreign editions in the bookcase where he kept them.

'These are all yours?'

'They've got my name on them,' he said.

'So you made it in the end.'

'If you call that making it.'

'Well, it is, isn't it? It's what you always wanted.'

'I suppose so. But sometimes I can't help feeling that I'm no more than a hack, turning out the same old book time and time again. With variations, of course. Always the same chief character, this Simpson of the Yard; never altering, never getting any older, sorting out the real fish from the red herrings and never failing to nail the murderer in the end, even if the villain has killed half a dozen more victims before this happy conclusion is reached. And he's such a prig, sneering at everybody with an IQ less than his and quoting Shakespeare at the drop of a hat. Have you ever met a policeman who quoted Shakespeare?'

'I've never met a policeman.'

'You're lucky.'

'Anyway,' she said, 'you invented him, didn't you?'

'Sometimes I wish I hadn't.'

'Now you're just being gloomy. I think you've done ever so well. I'm proud of you.'

'Well, that's something,' he said. And it cheered him to hear her say it. It gave him a feeling of warmth around the heart. 'One day,' he said, 'I'm going to write a real book.'

'Yes, darling,' she said, 'I'm sure you are.'

*

It was getting late when she said it was time for her to return to the hotel where she was staying.

'Do you have to?' he said.

She gave him the sort of glance which might have been part of her stage repertoire. 'Are you suggesting,' she asked, 'what I think you're suggesting?'

'I should think it's highly probable – if you're thinking what I think you're thinking I'm suggesting.'

She laughed, with a delicious gurgle in her throat. 'This is becoming far too complicated. Am I to take it that you're inviting me to stay the night?'

'Yes, I am.'

'Then I accept. I should have been most disappointed if you had not.'

Chapter Twenty-Nine – MURDER

She checked out from her hotel the next day and moved in with him. It seemed the natural thing to do. It was like those days in the Lakoses' house, and yet it was not like them. The Lakoses were dead and they had both experienced much since that earlier time. A war had intervened between those days and these, and much else besides. They could never again be the persons they had been then. People change with the years, but what had not changed with them was the passion they felt for each other. There had been an interruption, but that was all. Now they were together again and it was like a renewal of living.

'We've got so much to make up for,' Angela said.

He knew what she meant. He felt the same way. There had been too many lost years.

But they could not be together all the time. They both had business matters to attend to. It appeared that the new show would be going ahead and she had been engaged for a leading role. It would take up a lot of her time, but at least it meant that she would stay in London and he would be able to see her on the stage whenever he wished.

*

One evening she brought up the subject of marriage. It was something they had never talked about, though it had been in Sterne's mind. Now it appeared that it had been in hers also.

'I'm twenty-nine,' she said, 'and I think it's time I had some children.'

It took him rather by surprise. She had never previously mentioned any desire to start a family.

'So,' he said, 'you're looking for a father for the brood?'

'That's about it.'

'And you've picked on me?'

'Can you think of anyone better?'

'Now that you mention it, no. Offhand, I can't.'

'So it's settled then?'

'If that's what you want.'

'Don't you?'

It was something he had never thought much about, but now that she had mentioned it he found that he rather liked the idea. They would need a larger residence of course. You couldn't raise a family in a one-bedroom maisonette. But that could be arranged. The money was there.

'Well, yes,' he said. 'Come to think of it, I do.'

'And we'll get married?'

'So you want that too?'

'Of course.'

So it appeared that one failure in that line had not put her off. She was prepared to have another try. And maybe this time it really would work. He hoped so, and believed it would.

'I think,' he said, 'we should go down east tomorrow and break the news to your parents.'

She agreed that this would be a good idea. 'I wonder how they'll take it.'

'They'll be delighted.'

'Are you sure of that?'

'Oh yes,' he said, 'I'm sure.'

And after a little while he said: 'There's likewise a wind on the heath.'

She stared at him. 'Now what are you babbling about? What wind? What heath?'

'Never mind,' he said. And then: 'Life is very sweet, brother. Who would wish to die?'

Again she stared at him. 'Have you gone crazy? I'm not your brother.'

'No, you aren't,' he said. 'And I can't begin to tell you how glad I am about that.'

*

He was right about the Maggses. He had never seen two people more delighted. Alfie brought out a bottle of champagne he had been saving up for just such an occasion and Queenie laid on a meal to beat anything that Sterne had previously enjoyed in the room above the greengrocery.

'This is the 'appiest day of my life,' Alfie said. And then he looked at Queenie and added: 'Bar one.'

Angela laughed and said: 'You just saved your skin there, Dad.'

Queenie said: 'He's a little bit tiddly, that's what it is. It's the champagne gone to his head.'

'No,' Alfie said, 'you're wrong, old girl. I'm just intoxicated with joy.'

'See what I mean?' she said. 'See what I mean?'

*

It was three days later when Sterne noticed a headline on the front page of the morning paper. It read: 'MAN ARRESTED ON DOUBLE MURDER CHARGE.'

He scanned the report with growing interest and gathered that a man named Judas Raven, a known gangster, had been arrested and charged with the murder of another man named Les Grannidge and a woman named Annie Siggers. It appeared that Siggers had until recently been living with Raven, but had left him and paired up with Grannidge, a suspected drug dealer who lived in an old house in Bethnal Green. A neighbour had heard shots late at night and had seen a car driving away. He had entered Grannidge's house and had found the drug dealer dead from shotgun wounds and the woman, Siggers, lying nearby with multiple stab wounds, probably inflicted with a knife. The neighbour was horrified by what he saw. He said there was blood everywhere and it was 'like a madman had done the job'.

Raven had been arrested at his home some time later. He had made no attempt to get away. He had even taken the sawn-off shotgun and the bloodstained knife back to his house, where they were found by the police.

Sterne passed the paper to Angela, and she read the report. When she had finished reading it she put the paper down and looked at him, wide-eyed, the colour all gone from her cheeks.

'Oh God,' she said. 'It could have been you.'

He knew what she meant. All those years ago in a similar situation. A man named Judas Raven – a madman.

'And you,' he said.

'Both of us.'

'Yes, both of us.'

They were silent for a while, thinking what might have happened if she had not walked out on him that fateful day in 1939.

Then he said: 'But it wasn't.'

Printed in Great Britain
by Amazon